LUCAS LIGHTFOOT
and the
WATER TOMB

By Hugo Haselhuhn
and Luke Cowdell
Illustrated by Heather Cowdell

Lucas Lightfoot and the Water Tomb

Published by Haselhuhn Design Inc.

Paso Robles, California

Copyright © 2014 by Hugo Haselhuhn

ISBN: 978-0-9912439-2-1

Library of Congress Control Number: 2014921754

Books by Hugo Haselhuhn and Luke Cowdell

Lucas Lightfoot and the Fire Crystal (2013)

Lucas Lightfoot and the Water Tomb (2014)

Lucas Lightfoot and the Sun Stone (2015)

Cover art by Laurel Palmer

Cover Layout Design by Heather Cowdell

The text type is 12-pt. Maiandra GD

Epigrams at the beginning of each chapter are quotes selected from the *Book of Prescottian Wisdom*.

Author's notes and comments about Lucas Lightfoot

Why do I write? It began as a way to help a grandson achieve a dream. As I continue to write, it is because I want to improve the lives of children. Throughout the story, my goal is to teach the importance of choice and accountability, the value of learning and improving the mind, importance of attitude and belief in one's ability to help others. Integrity and honesty are still valuable traits to develop and hold dear. There is value in love, understanding and gratitude in our lives. These values are critical for a rising generation that is bombarded with anti-heroes that exemplify the opposite traits of selfishness, falsehoods, power-seeking and bullying. The lessons are conveyed just beneath the natural conversations of the characters while the reader is drawn into the excitement that comes with the challenges and adventures in the story. I marvel as I watch children read the story and get excited as they are caught up in the adventure and excitement. One of the greatest compliments I have yet heard about the book, is the children are "playing Lucas Lightfoot" on the playground. If I can enlighten a child and take them on an adventure they enjoy again and again, I feel successful in my writing. Why do I write? I write to change the world, one child at a time.

There are no famous people endorsing the Lucas Lightfoot series, but there are a number of parents,

Acknowledgements

If you read *Lucas Lightfoot and the First Crystal*, you will remember that my grandson and I started this series because of his desire to write a "chapter book." I am grateful to Luke and his mother, Heather Cowdell, who encouraged her son to accomplish his dreams. In this story, the adventure continues for Lucas Lightfoot with elements from the childhood of a grandfather and his grandson. Luke and I collaborated on general ideas for the story. Luke told me where he wanted to go and I provided the road, created the characters and painted the scenery along the road they traveled.

I am thankful to my daughter Heather, who is the artistic talent behind the illustrations. She helps to bring the story to life with her pictures. I am thankful to Laurel Palmer who captured the essence of the story in the cover artwork.

I invited three young friends to read the story aloud so I could evaluate language and sentence structure. Mary, Ethan and Mason provided the needed feedback to fine tune the story. I am grateful to Janice Paxman for the careful technical editing for a polished manuscript.

To connect with readers, I invited them into the story with their suggestions for a new power for Lucas Lightfoot. There were many great suggestions, and after careful consideration, the authors selected the top suggestion. Special thanks go out to Mabel, Brittney, Kendall and Trenton for suggesting the power to heal. Look for these names as characters in the book.

A special thanks to my wife Lydia, who encouraged me throughout the writing by reminding me that the readers will be children and to write for them.

teachers and children that have something to say and their honest endorsements mean so much more to us.

<u>Lucas Lightfoot and the Water Tomb</u>

"Hugo Haselhuhn has done it again. He has invoked young Lucas to represent the power of positive over the darkness of negativity and evil. I was hooked from the start with the vivid descriptions, intrigue of a talking chameleon guiding the young hero, and page turning suspense. As a parent and teacher, I was captured by the action and integrity. The book speaks to children. It is relatable. Kids love powers and super heroes. Better yet, parents and teachers are attracted to this young book hero who has powers that are activated and strengthened by virtues. The power of communication and understanding of dialogue between light bearer and animal is a real draw for kids. Kids love animals. The author has a knack for kid connection. *Lucas Lightfoot and the Water Tomb* is sure to engage the audience of today's youth while teaching lessons throughout the plot and building character simultaneously. It is like the perfect ice cream sundae with goodness and unselfish acts as the nuts and cherry on top. This book is an adventurous treat for children and adults alike. Find a young friend and read it together."

Sandi Moore ~ 3rd Grade Teacher
Templeton, CA

"In this suspenseful sequel to *Lucas Lightfoot and the Fire Crystal*, the reader joins Lucas in his continuing quest to attain the virtue of a Light Bearer. My students used adjectives like "hypnotizing," mysterious," and superb" to describe the story they previewed. Young readers will be captivated by the plot of the story, but they won't fail to recognize that the goodness in Lucas's

heart is the true source of his power. This book is perfectly suited for the minds and hearts of children."
Cindy Miller ~ 3rd Grade Teacher
Templeton, CA

Lucas Lightfoot and the Fire Crystal

"*Lucas Lightfoot and the Fire Crystal* is a lovely tale about the adventures of Lucas and his chameleon. As a teacher, I have enjoyed this story immensely because it has a positive message and is relatable to my students. Sharing it with my students has opened the door for interesting, deep conversations. My students find the story amazing and fun!"
Crystal Romans ~ 5th Grade Teacher
Herriman, UT

"I love the positive messages about virtue, attitude and choices. It's perfect and my kids love it. In fact, I love when I hear them talk about why it's good to be good in the way we just read."
Darren E. ~ Santa Monica, CA

"It was a really good book. I learned a couple things; I learned to trust other people and always be honest just like Lucas and Hailey. My favorite part of the book was when Hailey finds out that Lucas can fly, stop time, and be invisible. I liked this because sometimes in my life I wish I was able to fly, or be invisible for millions of reasons, like at school or sometimes during activities."
Ben B., (10 year old) – Dana Point, CA

"The book is very exciting with good characters and an intriguing plot. Even if there wasn't a deeper meaning to everything, it would still stand on its own.

Important skills and character traits are taught through the experiences of the main character. It is magical."
Tim M. ~ Templeton, CA

"This is a very delightful and amazing book. The story line is captivating and very original. Our 8-year-old son has reread the book five times and I overheard him say that he and friends at school are playing Lucas Lightfoot on the play ground and using "their power" for good."
Lenny Z. ~ Paso Robles, CA

"I sat down with my kids (aged 6 and 9 yrs old) to read them a chapter or two. After each chapter they cheered for more. We read the entire book cover to cover in one sitting. It's a fun story with some good values and wisdom woven in too."
Trevor L. ~ Templeton, CA

"Lucas Lightfoot and the Fire Crystal was one of those stories that I would have loved to read as a kid. Lucas and his magical chameleon set out on adventures that are enjoyable while teaching valuable lessons. It's sometimes difficult for a child to choose the right thing when so many possibilities lie in front of them. Lucas Lightfoot presents those choices and their solutions in a way that wasn't heavy handed. This book will appeal to boys and girls and is a great conversation starter."
Karen @ For What It's Worth

TABLE OF CONTENTS

ONE

NOT ALONE ANY MORE

A friend is someone who understands your past, believes in your future, and accepts you just the way you are.

The sky was very blue that day in late May and the white clouds reminded Lucas of popcorn. It was sunny, that is, until a shadow started covering the backyard at the home of Lucas's grandfather. Thinking the shadow was from one of the clouds, Lucas looked up to see a dark shape covering the sun. It wasn't a cloud at all but a dark form that quickly came down on top of Lucas and enclosed him in a dark mist. Lucas started shivering as he was surrounded by the shape. His nose was attacked by the smell of rotten eggs, and he found it very difficult to breathe. He yelled to his grandfather, but no sound came out of his mouth. Each breath caused his nose and throat to hurt like the stings of a thousand bees. Lucas felt as if he were bound by an invisible rope. He couldn't move his arms to fight off his attacker or move his feet to run. He felt himself being lifted off the ground and being pulled away. His grandfather turned around and reached out for Lucas, but it was too late. Lucas saw his grandfather and the backyard getting smaller as he felt himself being pulled up and away very fast. The last thing Lucas remembered was seeing Prescott on his grandfather's shoulder, and there was a bright glow coming from Prescott's collar. After that, everything went dark.

(One hour earlier, before the disappearance of Lucas.)

Lucas Lightfoot had traveled to the California Central Coast with his family to visit his grandparents just a few days after the fire at school. The school was shut down because of the fire investigation, and the students were let out a week early for summer vacation. It was good to get away from all of the attention of the fire and his heroic rescue of Anna. Sometimes he thought that life would be easier if he could go back to being a normal boy with a normal life. But he had met Prescott, a magical chameleon, that fateful day on the sidewalk, and things would never be the same again.

Prescott was more than a magical chameleon. He had become Lucas's friend and mentor. Lucas trusted Prescott, and together they had some pretty awesome adventures. Lucas had talked his parents into bringing Prescott on the trip to visit his grandparents. On Saturday afternoon, Lucas was in his grandpa's backyard with Prescott while the rest of the family had walked over to his aunt's house. That was just the way he wanted it.

"Lucas, what did you want to talk about?" asked Grandpa Jack as he stepped out onto the patio. Prescott had told Lucas during the car ride that he could tell his grandfather about the Power Ring because he would understand. Lucas was glad to tell his grandpa about the power he had been given and to show him the ring.

"Grandpa, I need to talk to you about something and I hope you don't think I am too crazy," said Lucas.

"Lucas, I have lived long enough to know that things are not always as they appear. And whatever you have to say, you know that I will not think that you are crazy," said Grandpa.

"I know," said Lucas, "that's why I want to talk with you about Prescott, but first I have some questions. What is magic and is it bad?"

"Well, magic is often linked to entertainment and show business, but I don't think that's what you had in mind," said Grandpa. "Are you talking about someone being able to do things by a supernatural power?"

"Yes. I'm talking about doing something that cannot be explained," said Lucas.

Grandpa thought a moment and said, "If you were to show a flashlight or cell phone or any new invention to someone from the 1700's, they would think that it is magic. Supernatural things that we do not understand are often called magic."

"Grandpa, what would you think of me if I told you that I had something that gives me special powers, sort of like magic?" asked Lucas.

"What kind of powers?" asked Grandpa.

"Well," said Lucas, "the power to stop time, or to be invisible, or to move things with my mind just by thinking."

"I see," said Grandpa, "and what gives you these powers?"

"I have a Power Ring. Well, it is actually more like a disk, but it gives me the power to be invisible or to move things with my mind," said Lucas.

"You mean you have the power of telekinesis?" asked Grandpa.

"Yes, and the power to stop time," said Lucas.

"Does that mean you can stop time for me so I don't get any older?" asked Grandpa

"I don't think so," said Lucas laughing.

"Where did you get this Power Ring?" asked Grandpa.

"Now you are really going to think I am crazy," said Lucas. "I got it from Prescott."

"I see," said Grandpa. "And how did Prescott give you these powers?"

Lucas told his grandpa how he had found Prescott on the sidewalk, and about meeting the woman with the green eyes who gave him the book in which he had found the Power Ring. He also told him some of the things he had been able to do with the ring, including the incident with the fire at school.

"May I see the ring?" asked Grandpa.

"Here it is," said Lucas as he pulled it from his pocket and handed it to his grandfather. "Mom and Dad know about the ring, but they don't know about the power it has or what I have been able to do with the help of the ring."

Lucas explained what some of the symbols represented and how they worked. He also told his grandfather how he helped Prescott find the crystal and return it to the ring to make it work.

"Grandpa," said Lucas, "Prescott told me that the ring can only be used for doing good things and if I try to use it for something wrong, it will stop working. As long as I have virtue in my life and have positive thoughts, the ring works for good. You probably think that I am a little crazy for saying this, but I am able to talk with Prescott."

"How do you talk with Prescott? Does he have a special language?" asked Grandpa with a grin on his face.

"I am able to talk to Prescott by thinking. He can hear my thoughts. When Prescott talks to me, I can hear his words as if they were thoughts in my head. And there is no special language. He just talks to me in English," said Lucas.

"Lucas, if the ring can only be used for good and works by the power of virtue, then it seems like whatever you do with the ring is good, and whether you call it magic or some other name, it's still good. It must be a challenge for you to have this knowledge and power. I'm sure that if Prescott chose you, it was for a very good reason."

Lucas thought quickly about what he had said to his grandfather during the last twenty minutes, but he could not remember saying that Prescott had chosen him.

"Wait a minute!" exclaimed Lucas. "How did you know that Prescott chose me? I haven't told anyone that."

"Well how do you think I know? Prescott told me this morning. In fact we had a very wonderful conversation about you," said Grandpa.

"You, you mean," stuttered Lucas, "you can hear Prescott's thoughts too?"

"Yes, I can," replied Grandpa Jack.

"Can you hear my thoughts?" asked Lucas with concern.

Grandpa replied, "No, I can't. Prescott has the ability to project his thoughts to whomever he wants, and he can hear their thoughts. Mental telepathy is the only way that he has to communicate with you."

Lucas was both excited and relieved to know that there was someone else that could understand what he was going through. It was really nice to know that he was not alone or crazy!

Lucas and his grandpa both heard Prescott say, *"Gotcha!"* They looked over at Prescott who was on the lawn just a few feet away. Prescott was obviously chewing on some bug he had just captured.

"Lucas, would you like to get some big crickets for Prescott?" asked Grandpa. Before Lucas could answer, they both heard Prescott say, *"Of course he would!"*

"Go look in the refrigerator and bring me the white Chinese take-out box," said Grandpa. "I had heard that you were bringing Prescott so I bought some big crickets for him."

"That was very kind. Thank you," said Prescott.

As Lucas went into the house, he was reminded again that Prescott was always very grateful for whatever was given to him. Maybe that was another lesson for Lucas. He should remember to be grateful for the gifts in his life. Lucas went to the refrigerator to look for the white box and wondered if Grandpa was trying to keep the crickets fresh.

While he was gone, Grandpa Jack asked, "Prescott, would you mind kissing Lucas?"

Prescott replied, *"I know where this is going, and I do not mind at all. In fact, it will be fun for Lucas and it will be lunch for me."*

Lucas returned with the white box and asked, "Why did you put the crickets in the refrigerator?"

"I wanted to teach you a new trick that involves you, Prescott and a cricket," said Grandpa. "The cold crickets will not be moving fast. I want you to pick one and put it in your hand and hold it about a foot away from Prescott."

Lucas did as his grandpa instructed and held the motionless cricket in the palm of his hand near Prescott. Prescott didn't wait for an invitation to snatch the cricket. His long tongue tickled Lucas's hand as the cricket quickly disappeared.

"Thank you. That was very tasty," said Prescott as he was chewing on the cricket.

Lucas broke into a grin when he realized that Prescott was able to eat a cricket and talk at the same time. His mom had always told him not to talk with food in his mouth. Now he and Prescott could chew and talk at the same time.

After Prescott had finished the first cricket, Lucas got out another one.

His grandpa said, "This time I want you to put the cricket between your lips."

"Are you kidding?" asked Lucas.

"Just try it," encouraged Grandpa.

Lucas hesitantly placed the cricket between his lips and moved closer to Prescott.

Prescott said, *"Be very still and just trust me. I am very good at this."*

In an instant, Prescott's moist tongue brushed against Lucas's lips and the cricket was gone.

"Now," said Grandpa, "I bet you are the only boy at school that can say that you have been kissed by a chameleon. Lucas, I want you to remember that if you ever need us, we are here and you are not alone."

"It's been really hard to keep this secret to myself, and I'm glad to know that you can hear Prescott too." said Lucas.

"Grandpa," said Lucas, "you haven't told me how you can hear Prescott."

"Jack," said Prescott, *"It's time to go inside before Rebulus comes and Lucas learns firsthand about the dark force."*

"I agree," said Grandpa Jack. Without hesitation, he picked up Prescott, grabbed Lucas's hand, and they went into the house. Once inside, Lucas turned around to look out the window and saw a dark shadow move across the back lawn. It hesitated at the fence then quickly disappeared. Lucas looked at the lawn and saw a strip of brown grass that had been green just moments before.

TWO

REBULUS THE LIGHT THIEF

Our principles are the only line between order and chaos.

"Grandpa, what was that shadow?" asked Lucas, "Why did we have to come inside?"

"Just a minute, Lucas," said Grandpa. "Prescott, why do you think that Rebulus was here?"

"I have not seen him in years," replied Prescott. *"But it is not like him to forget us and disappear. I suspect that he has learned there is to be a new Light Bearer and this would disrupt his plans."*

"Grandpa, what are you guys talking about and what's a Light Bearer?" pleaded Lucas.

Grandpa turned to Lucas with a serious look and said, "Prescott has been looking for new Light Bearers to train, and he has chosen you. You have the opportunity to accept that responsibility if you are willing to be trained by him. The training will take some time before you develop all the skills to assume the responsibilities of a Light Bearer."

"But what is a Light Bearer?" asked Lucas again.

"A Light Bearer is someone who has a combination of virtue, love, and the courage to choose correct paths in life. He becomes a beacon of light to those around him. A Light Bearer seeks for the good in others and leads by example. A Light Bearer does just what the name implies - brings light to the world and dispels the darkness," said Grandpa.

"Why was I chosen?" asked Lucas.

Grandpa explained, "You were chosen because of your character and your willingness to choose right over wrong. This can be your destiny, but you must choose. There are others who have passed up the opportunity to be a Light Bearer and chose a different path. If you decide to be a Light Bearer and choose that path, there are many whose lives will be better because they have seen your light."

Grandpa had a concerned look on his face as he said, "You will find that the path of a Light Bearer will be difficult, especially in a world where honesty and virtue are not valued. On that path you may be tempted to be dishonest. But that path will also lead to great happiness. There may be others, even some of your friends who will become Light Bearers as well."

"What was that shadow I saw in the backyard? What did you call it?" asked Lucas.

Prescott replied, "*Rebulus the Light Thief is what we call him. He was first encountered by a Light Bearer at Lake Avernus near Naples, Italy. Some of the stories about the lake suggest that it has poisonous vapors. Rebulus the Light Thief wants to destroy as many Light Bearers as possible,*" said Prescott.

"I did not see anyone, only a dark cloud," said Lucas.

"He was inside the cloud," said Prescott. "He uses the poisonous cloud surrounding him to bind his victim and then he sucks the light out of them."

"Was he after me?" asked Lucas.

"I am afraid he was," replied Prescott. "He feels compelled to attack all Light Bearers. Your grandfather can explain the story about Rebulus?

"Sure," replied Jack. "As the legend goes, Rebulus was the son of a woman who was a Light Bearer and a demon. When Rebulus was born, he was so ugly that he did not look human. His mother had been deceived by the demon. She regretted what she had done and in her anguish, she threw herself and Rebulus into Lake Avernus to drown. His demon father rescued the baby but let the mother die. The demon filled Rebulus with lies and a hatred for all Light Bearers. Rebulus was given the power to suck light out of humans. All of us have a light within us but Rebulus is especially eager to attack the young Light Bearers. As you develop your own strength and increase the light power within you, Rebulus will have no influence or control over you."

"Grandpa, could he have followed us inside the house?" asked Lucas.

"No. I have placed a shield on the house to prevent any evil or darkness from entering the house," replied Grandpa.

"We should use that shield to prevent Rebulus from having any influence on Lucas until his power increases and is strengthened," said Prescott.

"That's a great idea," said Grandpa.

"What's a shield?" asked Lucas.

"It is like having an invisible bubble or shield around you for protection against those like Rebulus and his kind," said Prescott.

"You mean there are others?" asked Lucas.

"Yes, too many to count," said Prescott. *"In fact, you will find that there are people all around that are influenced by dark forces like Rebulus, but they do not know that they are being controlled or influenced to do evil."*

"Lucas," said Grandpa, "As you get older, you will find that there are people that just seem to drain energy from you. These people need your energy to survive. They are eager to share their problems with you so you will feel sorry for them. Most often they just want attention. You will know who these people are because you feel tired after talking with them."

"I have heard Mom say that a neighbor tends to suck the life out of her with all of her problems," said Lucas. "Is that what you mean?"

"That's right, Lucas," said Grandpa. "Some of these people have chaos in their lives and it is often because of the poor choices they have made. They seem to make every situation a confusing mess."

Prescott cautioned, *"Lucas, you will need to rely on your heart to know the difference between people with chaos and those that may be controlled by a dark force such as Rebulus and his kind. Those that have some darkness in them will seek to destroy you and your light. It is time we give you a little extra protection with an invisible shield."*

With that, Prescott's collar started to glow brightly until Prescott, Lucas, and Grandpa Jack were encircled by a ball of light. Lucas felt like he might have been floating in air and he felt a warm sensation all over, like being on the beach with a warm breeze. He heard a sound like rushing water. Lucas was enjoying the sensation of floating on a warm breeze. He did not know if it was seconds, minutes or hours, but after some time had passed, the light quickly retreated back to Prescott's collar.

Lucas found himself sitting at the kitchen table playing checkers with Grandpa when his mom walked in the front door.

"Hi Papa," said Lucas's mother Hannah, "why didn't you answer the phone?"

"Sorry Hannah," said Grandpa Jack, "we were outside feeding Prescott some crickets."

Hannah continued, "We've all been invited to Sophie's house. Her husband is making his famous tri-tip for dinner."

Grandpa replied, "Okay. Lucas and I will walk over in a few minutes as soon as he wins this game of checkers."

Hannah left and Lucas was sitting at the table feeling a little confused. He was playing checkers with his grandpa, but he didn't remember coming inside the house. He remembered Prescott snatching a cold cricket out of his mouth and eating it.

In his mind, Grandpa Jack privately asked Prescott, "Prescott, *did you block Lucas's memory of the visit from Rebulus?*"

"I did." replied Prescott. *"I used the power of time jumping to bring Lucas back to an hour before Rebulus grabbed him. I also thought that it would be best to remove the memory of that experience as well."*

"That's probably a wise choice," said Grandpa.

"His memory will come back when the time is right, when he needs to protect himself," replied Prescott.

"Grandpa, when did we come in the house and start playing checkers?" asked Lucas. "The last thing I remember is being outside with you and Prescott."

"We came inside the house after feeding Prescott, and we were playing checkers when your mom came over," replied Grandpa Jack. "So now that you have won the game, let's walk over to Aunt Sophie's house for the tri-tip barbeque."

Lucas was still a little confused, but being confused was often normal since finding Prescott. After putting Prescott in his cage, Lucas grabbed his hat and he and Grandpa stepped outside.

"That's a great looking hat," said Grandpa. "That looks like Prescott on your hat."

"Thanks," said Lucas. "It is Prescott. Mom has a special sewing machine and she embroidered a picture of Prescott on to the hat. That way, wherever I go, I can put on my hat and take Prescott with me. It is kind of like having him in my head all of the time reminding me what's right and wrong."

Grandpa Jack lived at the edge of the city. The other side of the street was county property with a horse ranch. As Lucas and his grandpa walked along the road, Lucas noticed that there were eight vultures sitting on the fence.

"Hey, Grandpa," said Lucas, "Look at those red-headed vultures. That's weird! They're all sitting about five feet apart, and it looks like they're watching us. They don't think we are going to be their dinner, do they?"

"No, they are probably waiting for some animal to die before they start eating," replied Grandpa. "Vultures eat meat off of animals that have died. Most people think vultures are disgusting, but they have an important job to do. They eat animals that have died and help prevent the spread of disease from the dead animals."

"I had always thought that vultures were disgusting. Now that I know they have a special job to do, I guess I will never look at vultures as bad anymore," said Lucas.

Just then, Lucas and Grandpa Jack saw a dark cloud floating down the hill behind the vultures. The horses nearby were spooked and started running back to the stables. Lucas thought that he had seen something like that before and a chill ran down his back. Grandpa Jack quickly raised his arm in an arc toward the vultures on the fence. Immediately all of the huge birds began flapping their wings at once and flew off of the fence. As if on cue, they all turned around and started flying directly into the dark cloud. As they flew directly into the cloud, it dissolved and disappeared.

"Wow! Did you see that, Grandpa?" exclaimed Lucas. "Wait a minute! Did you do that?"

"One of the reasons you wanted to talk with me today about Prescott is that you trusted me," said Grandpa. "You thought that I would understand what you wanted to tell me. Lucas, you need to know I am a Light Bearer like you. What you just witnessed was something taught to me by a Master Light Bearer and you will be able to learn how to do what I just did."

"How did you do that, Grandpa?" asked Lucas.

Grandpa replied, "You are able to talk with Prescott by using your mind. The power of mental telepathy can be used to speak with other animals as well. I spoke to the vultures in my mind and thanked them for their service. I then asked them to fly directly into the dark cloud and scatter it."

"Does that mean I will have the ability to speak with animals?" asked Lucas excitedly.

"Yes, you will, but I will let Prescott teach you," said Grandpa.

"Were you afraid when that black cloud came toward us?" asked Lucas.

"Well, I could have been afraid, but I have learned to focus on my courage by having positive thoughts and faith that I can accomplish what is needed," said Grandpa.

"How do you do that? How do you focus on your courage?" asked Lucas.

"If I focus on my fear of failing and think about everything that can go wrong, then that is what tends to happen. If I focus on and nourish my courage, and think about how I want the situation to end, then that is what usually happens. Does that make sense?" asked Grandpa.

"I guess so," replied Lucas.

"Fear will cloud your mind and make your thoughts confusing. You must learn to suppress fear and control your thoughts. Having courage doesn't mean you don't have fear or you're not afraid. It means you overcome your fear by focusing on whatever it is that you want to accomplish. The brave man might feel fear but he has learned to conquer his fear. If you focus on fear it gets stronger. When you focus on having courage, your courage grows stronger," said Grandpa.

"So if I ignore my fear, it gets weaker, and if I nourish my courage, it gets stronger?" asked Lucas.

"That's right," said Grandpa. "It all begins and ends in your mind. What you give power to will have power over you. But being brave is not enough. You need to be smart as well. Being brave and foolish will get you into trouble. It's important to be brave and smart. Look at your surroundings to determine if there are things in nature that can help you."

"You mean like the vultures were part of nature?" asked Lucas.

"Exactly," said Grandpa. "The elements in nature could be things like rocks or water or living things like the vultures or other animals. Lucas, what you have seen today must be kept just between you and me. Can you do that for me?"

"Sure, Grandpa, it's our secret," said Lucas. "Oh, I almost forgot, happy birthday."

"Let's keep that a secret, too," said Grandpa laughing. "All right, number-one grandson, let's go get our tri-tip dinner and some birthday cake."

THREE
THE LIGHT BEARER

A life lived with integrity is the light to guide fellow travelers.

Lucas called Hailey the night he returned home from his grandparents and arranged to meet her at the garden at ten o'clock the next morning. Even though the school had closed because of the fire, Lucas thought a good place to meet Hailey was at the school garden. Much of the produce the students grew went to a local food bank and most of it had been harvested. There were still some vegetables on the vines, and Lucas was going to pick some tomatoes and cucumbers for an elderly neighbor.

Hailey walked over to the school and was waiting when Lucas arrived on his bike. Hailey helped Lucas fill one bag with the ripe vegetables, and then they went to sit on a nearby bench to talk.

"Okay," said Hailey, "you have kept me waiting all weekend. What was it that you couldn't tell me until now?"

"Remember, you promised to keep everything I say a secret. I need you to promise that what I tell you will never be repeated. I have not even told my parents yet," said Lucas.

"We did a pinky swear, remember? I meant what I said earlier. Your secret is safe with me," said Hailey.

Lucas had really hoped this was true. On the trip home from his grandpa's house, Lucas was dozing. Somewhere between awake and asleep, he thought about the conversation with his grandpa and Prescott that he was a Light Bearer. He was not sure what it all meant, but when he asked Prescott, he was told, "all in good time." He wanted more answers than Prescott was willing to give. He also remembered that his grandpa had said that some of his friends would be Light Bearers as well. Although Prescott did not tell him directly, Lucas figured that the reason Prescott agreed to let him tell Hailey was that she might be a Light Bearer like himself.

"Okay," said Lucas, "Don't think that I am crazy for the things that I will tell you."

"I promise," said Hailey.

For the next hour Lucas told Hailey about finding Prescott on the sidewalk, about the Power Ring and about the strange woman that had given Prescott to him. Lucas explained where he and Prescott found the crystal and his encounter with Kevin under the bridge. He also explained how he used the Power Ring to stop time and save her from the trash truck. He told her how had to overcome his fear of fire and use the power of telekinesis to save Anna from the school fire.

"So far, Prescott has taught me how to use the Power Ring to become invisible, to move things with my mind and to stop time. There are other powers that are on the ring, but I cannot use them yet," said Lucas.

"I knew there was something strange about the way you've been acting," said Hailey.

"What do you mean by strange?" asked Lucas.

"Oh! I don't mean strange like weird, but, you know, you just seemed different," said Hailey.

"Different how?" asked Lucas.

"I mean, you are still nice, but you just seem different, in a good way though. You seem to be more confident, and I have noticed that you are kinder to everyone," said Hailey.

"Did you think I wasn't kind before?" asked Lucas.

"That's not what I meant," said Hailey. "You seem to be more kind than you were before. And I don't think you are crazy because I have seen what you can do and I believe you."

Lucas said, "I still do not understand how these powers work. It has something to do with having an honest heart and virtue. The Fire Crystal in the Power Ring helps to magnify the power of my thoughts. I just know if I use the ring for good, it works. If I use it for selfish reasons, it backfires."

"What do you mean it backfires?" asked Hailey.

"I tried using the Power Ring once as a short cut to gather up all the leaves and grass in the front yard. Instead, the leaves and grass formed into a miniature tornado in my front yard. It was moving around the yard and then it headed straight for the front door. I let go of the ring and the tornado stopped. I decided I should use the rake instead," said Lucas as they both laughed.

"Can I see the Power Ring?" asked Hailey.

"I will have to show you later. I left it at home in a safe place," replied Lucas.

"You said that Prescott talks with you?" asked Hailey.

"Well, yes, sort of. Prescott communicates just by thought. He hears what I am thinking and I hear his thoughts. Prescott has the ability to send his thoughts to anyone he wants to talk to," said Lucas.

"Isn't that called mental telepathy?" asked Hailey.

"Yes. When we were coming home from my grandparent's home yesterday, Prescott and I were having a conversation in the car, but no one else heard it. Prescott told me that when I have the Power Ring with me, he and I will be able to communicate even though we are miles apart. It has something to do with the link between the power ring and Prescott's collar," said Lucas.

"Are you able to hear my thoughts?" asked Hailey.

"No. I can't," assured Lucas.

"Well that's a relief!" giggled Hailey.

"Prescott also has the ability to talk with animals," said Lucas. "When I was walking Kevin's dog home, I heard the conversation between Prescott and Ranger."

"Can you talk with animals, too?" asked Hailey.

"No. Well, maybe yes. I don't know. I guess Prescott lets me listen in on conversations he has with other animals," said Lucas. "There is a symbol on the ring for mental telepathy. As soon as Prescott teaches me, I will have the power to hear what other people are thinking. I will also be able to send my thoughts to other people. That is how Prescott communicates."

"Does Prescott have a power ring, too?" asked Hailey.

"Well, sort of. When I brought Prescott to class, did you see his collar?"

"I did. It looked really cool. I was wondering about the symbols but didn't ask," said Hailey.

"Prescott's collar has the same symbols that are on the Power Ring. He uses his collar the same way I can use the Power Ring," said Lucas. "When I was visiting my grandparents, I found out that my grandpa also has the ability to hear Prescott's thoughts. My grandpa told me that I was going to be a Light Bearer but I am still trying to figure out what a Light Bearer is."

Just then Hailey started shivering even though they were sitting in the warm sunlight and said, "Did you feel that? What is that awful smell?"

Lucas felt it, too. There was something strangely familiar about that feeling and the smell of rotten eggs.

"Yes, I did," replied Lucas. "I think I felt the same thing when I was at my grandpa's house, but I can't remember why. Not only did it feel cold but it felt like something dark or evil."

Lucas was thinking about their conversation of Light Bearers and it occurred to him that they both felt the chill right after he had said "Light Bearer."

Hailey started to ask, "So what is a ..."

"Shhh," said Lucas quickly holding a finger to his lips. "I think we should not talk about what I just said. I think someone is listening."

"What do you mean," said Hailey as she looked around. "There's no one here."

"Hailey, there is no one that we can see, but I think that someone or something is here. I don't know who or what that was, but we both felt it, and until I can learn more from Prescott, I don't think we should talk about it," said Lucas.

Hailey reluctantly agreed. She didn't like the feeling she had when she shivered. It felt like some darkness had come over them.

"Maybe you are right," she said. "When you find out from Prescott, please let me know what it is and if we are in any danger."

FOUR

CONVERSATIONAL CANINE

If your friend could read your thoughts, would they still like to be with you?

Lucas and Hailey agreed not to speak about the Light Bearer until Lucas could learn more from Prescott. Lucas went home with his bag of vegetables for his neighbor, and Hailey went home feeling a little heavier with the burden of the information that Lucas had shared with her. In spite of this, she was happy she had a friend like Lucas and was able to share his secret. For some reason, she had a feeling that something exciting was going to happen. It was the same feeling of excitement she felt the day before going to Disneyland.

When Hailey got home, her mom asked, "How did the visit with Lucas go?"

"It was good. We talked, and I helped Lucas pick a bunch of tomatoes and cucumbers for an elderly neighbor that lives near him," said Hailey.

"What sort of things did you talk about?" asked her mother.

"We talked about his pet chameleon Prescott and about one of the boys at school that sometimes is a bully," said Hailey. "He also told me a little about his trip to visit his grandparent's home over the weekend."

"He seems like a nice boy, especially since he stopped you from being run over by that garbage truck. What did you hear about Lucas saving the little girl during the fire at school?" asked Hailey's mother.

"He told me that he went back to the classroom to get Prescott and then found Anna crying in her classroom. Mom, after you went back into the house, I continued watching the fire from our back fence. I did not see him go back to the class room to get Prescott, but I did see him bringing Anna from the burning building," said Hailey.

"He must be a very special young man," said Hailey's mother.

"He is special and kind of different, but in a good way. I guess Prescott must be very special too for Lucas to go back into the fire to get him," said Hailey.

Hailey's mother had noticed that her daughter seemed a little different after coming home from her time with Lucas, but she couldn't quite figure out exactly what it was.

"Hailey," said her mother, "I was thinking that we should invite Lucas and his family over for a barbeque to get to know the family a little better. What do you think about that?"

"I guess that would be okay," replied Hailey.

"All right, I will call Lucas's mother and see what day would be best for them," said her mother.

Hailey was wondering why her mother was so interested in meeting Lucas's family.

🐾 🐾 🐾

Lucas delivered the vegetables to his neighbor, Mrs. Allen, and went to get Prescott to see if he was willing to tell him more about the darkness he and Hailey felt that morning. The nice thing about talking with Prescott is that Lucas could be in his room and talk without ever opening his mouth to speak. He put a few crickets in the cage and put some fresh water in the bowl for Prescott.

"Thank you, Lucas," said Prescott.

Once again, Lucas was reminded that Prescott was always very polite and appreciative for everything. Lucas realized that he was beginning to recognize the blessings in his own life. Lucas lay down on his bed, closed his eyes and started a conversation with Prescott in his mind.

"Prescott, can you tell me more about the Light Bearer? When I was with Hailey, I told her about you and the Power Ring. I mentioned that you and Grandpa told me that I was a Light Bearer, and right afterward, we both felt cold and sensed something dark. It was almost a feeling of evil. What was that?" asked Lucas.

"Lucas, when we were at your grandfather's house and started talking about a Light Bearer, an evil darkness appeared and that is when we went into the house. I placed a shield around you to prevent it from harming you until you have the power to keep it away on your own. You and Hailey felt the presence of Rebulus. He is a dark power and

he does not want you or Hailey to become Light Bearers."

"You mean that Hailey is also a Light Bearer?" Lucas asked excitedly.

"Yes, she can be," said Prescott. *"You probably think that Hailey is a pretty girl, and she is pretty. But there is something more that you sensed about her. Am I right?"*

"Yes, but what is it?" asked Lucas.

"You each have the qualities and the character traits that make for a great Light Bearer. You see that in each other. There is a light in her eyes that sets her apart from others," said Prescott, *"and you have that same light. I think it is time that you learn to use another power on the ring."*

"Which one?" asked Lucas.

"I believe that you are ready for the ability to read other people's thoughts," said Prescott.

"But I can already do that. How about something fun like time jumping?" insisted Lucas.

"You can only hear my thoughts because I allow you to hear me. Let us work on mental telepathy. Once you have mastered that, we can

40

move on to something more 'fun' as you say. You can hear my thoughts because I am projecting them to you. With mental telepathy, you will be able to talk with others, but first they must invite you into their thoughts," said Prescott.

"What do mean by 'invite' me into their thoughts?" asked Lucas.

"You must ask them for permission to listen to their thoughts, and they must say yes. The symbol on the Power Ring is the straight line with the two arrows pointing inward. As you squeeze that symbol, you need to imagine a pipeline between your head and the person with whom you want to communicate," said Prescott.

Lucas asked hopefully, "Will I be able to talk with animals like you did with Ranger?"

"Yes, you will, except you do not need to ask permission. The animals will naturally accept communication from you," replied Prescott. "Pets such as dogs and most cats will be eager to talk with you. But with wild animals you will need to be a little more cautious. They will likely be afraid of you because you are coming into their environment, and it is not normal for them to talk with people."

"Will Hailey and I be able to use mental telepathy to talk?" asked Lucas.

"Yes. In fact, that will be the preferred method of communication, especially if you are going to talk about becoming a Light Bearer. Rebulus or any of the other dark forces cannot read your thoughts," said Prescott.

Lucas and Prescott had been friends long enough for Lucas to be able to recognize different expressions from Prescott. Lucas could see a very concerned look come over Prescott's face as he spoke.

"Listen carefully to what I have to say," warned Prescott. "I have a strong caution and warning for you. Do not ever invite communication with one of the dark forces."

"Why is that so dangerous?" asked Lucas.

"Once they get into your head, you may not be able to control your own thoughts or actions," said Prescott. "Remember this, Lucas. Never, ever start a mental communication with a dark force. They will speak nothing but lies of the blackest night."

"Okay, I hear you loud and clear," said Lucas.

"Lucas, we must continue this discussion later. There is someone coming to your house to see you," said Prescott.

"How do you know that?" asked Lucas.

"In time you will develop a sense of things that are about to happen once you master all of the powers on the ring. You need to go see who is at the door," said Prescott.

Lucas was just getting up off of the bed when the door bell rang. Lucas looked over at Prescott and nodded his head once acknowledging Prescott's unique skill. As Lucas got near the front door, his mother called to him telling him that someone was here to see him. Lucas saw Kevin and Ranger standing at the front door.

Kevin said, "Hi Lucas, can you come outside? I need to talk to you about my dog Ranger."

"Sure," said Lucas as he stepped outside and closed the door. "What is this about?"

The two boys stood outside on the small patio in front of Lucas's house with Ranger between them.

"Lucas," said Kevin, "I need some help. I am moving to Nevada for the summer to stay with my dad. He lives in an apartment that does not take dogs. My mom is working all of the time and she says that she cannot take care of my dog. I need to leave Ranger with someone I can trust, someone I know will take good care of him while I'm away. I know this is going to sound really strange, but last night I had a dream. I dreamed that Ranger was talking with me. He told me he wanted to live with you while I am away and that you would take care of him."

Lucas thought about his discussion with Prescott and mentally rotated the pointer on the Power Ring to the symbol for mental telepathy and squeezed it in his mind.

Lucas asked, *"Ranger, do you want to live with me while Kevin is away for the summer?"*

"Yes sir. My master is going away and you are my friend, too. Your lizard told me that I was to protect you like he does," replied Ranger.

Lucas tried hard to suppress his smile as he thought about this new found ability to talk with animals.

"To be honest Kevin, I have had some really strange dreams like that as well," said Lucas. "I don't think that your dream is weird at all."

Kevin asked, "Will you be able to take Ranger for the summer? I have several large bags of food for him so you will not have to spend any money. He is well-trained obedient dog."

"I have no doubt that Ranger will be obedient, but I need to ask my parents. We are going camping next month. If I can watch Ranger, would it be okay if we took him camping with us?" asked Lucas.

"Sure," said Kevin. "I don't think that would be a problem. Just make sure he's on a leash and doesn't run away. I should be back the week before school starts so you only need to take care of him for about two months".

"Let me talk to my parents and I will call you tonight," said Lucas.

"All right, thank you," said Kevin as he turned to leave.

As Kevin and Ranger walked toward the street, Lucas asked, *"Ranger, are you going to be a good dog for me?"*

Ranger looked back at Lucas and replied, *"Yes. I will be a very good dog."*

Lucas went into the house smiling. Later that night at dinner, Lucas asked if he could take care of

Kevin's dog for the summer. His parents agreed since it was only for two months. Lucas was happy because he was going to be able to talk to an animal. Even though Prescott was a chameleon, Lucas didn't think of him as an animal. Prescott seemed more like a wise old sage and was more human than some people.

FIVE

GREAT-GRANDMA ELLIE

When virtue ceases to be a nuisance and becomes our quest, in that moment we will be endowed with power.

A few days after Hailey and Lucas met at the school garden, Lucas was in his room reading when his mom walked in. Her eyes were red and he knew she had been crying.

"What's wrong?" asked Lucas.

"I just heard that my grandma is really sick and not doing well," said his mother.

Lucas knew that she was talking about Grandpa Jack's mother, Eleanor, but Lucas called her Grandma Ellie. He also knew that she was ninety-nine years old. She was very frail and had been sick for some time. She had seen many things in her life and he remembered seeing a picture of her in her army uniform after she had enlisted in the army during World War II. He thought that she and Prescott were about the same age.

Lucas's mother, Hannah, asked, "Would you like to go with me to visit her at the hospital?"

"Sure," said Lucas. "Can I bring Prescott?"

"Okay, but keep him out of sight in the shoulder pack," replied his mother.

Lucas's younger brother and sister were at his cousin's house playing, so it was just Lucas and his mom in the car when Lucas asked, "Is Grandma Ellie going to die?"

"I don't know for sure. I heard from the doctor that Grandma Ellie is not doing well," replied Lucas's mother.

When they got to Grandma Ellie's hospital room, they found her sleeping. They woke her up and she smiled and held Hannah's hand.

"Hello sweetie. I see you brought your special young man. Hello Lucas, I'm so glad you came to see me. How are you?" said Grandma Ellie.

"We're doing fine, but I heard that you are not doing so well," said Hannah.

"The doctors say that my heart is not working like it should. My roommate has been very sweet in telling me what to expect when I die," said Grandma Ellie.

Lucas looked over at the woman in the bed next to his great-grandma while his mom continued her conversation with Grandma Ellie. He was surprised to see the silver-haired woman with the green eyes smiling at him.

"*Hello, Lucas. I see you've brought Prescott with you inside your shoulder pack. How is he doing?*" asked Katrina.

Lucas realized that the woman was Katrina, the one that had given him Prescott. He started to answer and realized that she was speaking to his mind like Prescott. With the surprised look on Lucas's face, Katrina knew that he could hear her thoughts.

"*I see that Prescott has shown you how to listen to other people's thoughts,*" said Katrina.

Lucas replied without speaking out loud, "*Prescott is doing fine. You can hear my thoughts, too?*"

"*Yes, Lucas. Prescott and I have had many discussions about you becoming a Light Bearer, and I* believe that he has chosen wisely. I am sure that you read the words on the back of the Power Ring, 'virtue unlocks power.' Have you wondered why virtue unlocks power?" asked Katrina.

"Sure I've wondered. I think I know how the Power Ring works but not why," said Lucas. "Can you explain it to me?"

"Virtue and Integrity are like brothers in the same family. Integrity is the same as honesty or truthfulness," said Katrina.

"So how does virtue unlock power?" asked Lucas.

"Virtues are habits that give us the power to act with courage and strength. Having integrity will earn you respect and trust from most people. Having virtue in your life will cause others to look up to you and will help build a relationship of trust with them. They will see the light that is in you and will want to follow you," explained Katrina.

"What does this have to do with being a Light Bearer?" asked Lucas.

"Very simply stated, virtue and integrity guide a Light Bearer to do the right thing even when no one is watching. When virtue becomes your quest, in that moment, you will be endowed with power," said Katrina.

Lucas felt comfortable speaking to Katrina only by thoughts, and her explanation was easy to understand. Do the right thing, even when no one is watching.

"What did Grandma Ellie mean when she said that you have been telling her what to expect when she dies?" asked Lucas.

"Lucas, I am what some people might call an angel. I help people make the transition from this life to the next. Your Grandma Ellie has asked me several times why she is still here. I think it is so your family has time to say goodbye to her. Maybe there is something special she needs to tell you. I know many will be sad when she passes, but death is a part of living. I can see how much your mother loves her," said Katrina.

Lucas turned back to see his mother with tears in her eyes again and asked Prescott a question. "Prescott, is there any way I can use the Power Ring to make Grandma Ellie well again?"

Prescott answered with a question, "*What does your heart tell you?*"

Lucas remembered his instruction that he was not to use the Power Ring in a way that would change the course of history and answered, "*My heart says that I should do nothing and just love Grandma Ellie.*"

"*That is right,*" said Katrina. "*Many times we hold on to our loved ones when it is time for them to go. You will need to be strong for your mom and help her in any way you can when Ellie passes. Be sure to share the good memories. That is how we can honor and remember those who have passed from this life.*"

Lucas stood closer to his mother and held Grandma Ellie's hand and said, "I love you, Grandma Ellie."

"I love you, too. Be good for your mother," said Grandma Ellie.

"I promise I will," said Lucas.

Hannah and Grandma Ellie talked for a little while until she said that she was tired and needed to sleep. Lucas and his mom gave Grandma Ellie a hug and said their goodbyes.

As Lucas and his mother were walking to the car, he heard Grandma Ellie in his mind say, *"Thank you for visiting me today."*

Lucas should have been surprised to hear Grandma Ellie in his mind, but it just seemed so natural and he replied, *"You are welcome. It was nice to see you."*

Grandma Ellie then said, *"Lucas, remember, as a Light Bearer you must be stronger than the storm."*

"What do you mean, 'be stronger than the storm?'" asked Lucas.

Lucas heard Grandma Ellie whisper, *"You will know when the time comes. Goodbye Lucas."*

Lucas did not know exactly what she meant by being stronger than the storm, but he was determined to keep her comment tucked away in his heart until he understood her meaning. Maybe that is what Grandma Ellie needed to tell him. Lucas had a feeling that would be the last time he would see her before she died. Two days later his mom got the call that Grandma Ellie had passed away. Lucas thought that he was supposed to cry, but he didn't. He realized that Grandma Ellie had lived a long and exciting life. It was time for her to be relieved of the pain she had had for many years. Lucas understood that the memories of those we love are never more than a thought away and as long as there is a memory, they will always live on in our heart.

SIX

WATER CANNON

The belief that you hold creates the reality you experience.

Lucas and his family went to Hailey Sinclair's home for a barbeque about a week after Grandma Ellie's funeral. The fathers talked outside around the barbeque grill while the mothers chatted in the kitchen. Lucas's little brother and sister were in the playroom with Hailey's little sister. That left Lucas and Hailey to sit in the chairs by the pool on the side of the house away from listening ears.

"Prescott has told me how to use the Power Ring for mental telepathy with you," said Lucas.

"Do you have the Power Ring with you? Can I see it?" asked Hailey.

Lucas pulled the ring from his pocket and handed it to Hailey. She carefully held it in her hands and looked at all of the symbols. She rubbed her fingers over all of the indentations created by the symbols feeling each one thoughtfully.

At first the metallic ring was cool to the touch, but as she held it in her hand, it started to get warmer and she felt it begin to vibrate. Hailey held the inner disk and turned the outer ring around several times. She turned the ring over and slowly read the words engraved on the backside saying each word deliberately. "VIRTUE ... UNLOCKS ... POWER." Lucas watched her expression and wondered what was going through her mind. Then he realized he could find out.

"How does virtue unlock power?" asked Hailey.

"The power from the ring only works because of virtue, honesty and positive thoughts. Virtue is like having good behavior all the time. When virtue becomes our habit, we have the power to act with courage."

Lucas continued, "Hailey, before we can use the ring for mental telepathy, you have to give me permission to listen to your thoughts. You can take back that permission anytime."

"Lucas, I give you permission to listen to my thoughts," said Hailey.

With that, Hailey handed the ring back to Lucas, and he turned the pointer to the symbol with the line and the two arrows and squeezed the symbol. He then imagined that there was an invisible pipeline between his head and Hailey's head.

"Hailey, can you hear me?" asked Lucas.

He did not need her to answer. It was evident that she could hear him because she had the biggest smile on her face. The dimples in her cheeks came out and her eyes were a bright blue. Lucas immediately thought back to the first time he met

Katrina. When Katrina smiled at Lucas that day on the door step, she seemed to glow. Hailey had that same glow. Whether it was the afternoon sun filtering through the backyard trees and reflecting off her blond hair or some other reason, Lucas did not know. But Lucas thought that her glow might be an indication that she was a Light Bearer.

"Who is Katrina, and am I really glowing?" asked Hailey.

The questions startled Lucas and he realized that Hailey heard everything he was thinking.

"Katrina is the lady with the green eyes and the silver hair that gave Prescott to me," said Lucas. *"I'm sure that I told you about her."*

"You did, but I didn't remember that her name was Katrina." replied Hailey.

Lucas realized the danger of being able to listen in on the thoughts of other people and decided that they needed to come to an agreement.

"You are probably right," said Hailey. *"We need to have an agreement that we will only think kind thoughts about one another and not keep secrets."*

"Agreed," said Lucas. "*It is pretty hard to keep a secret when our thoughts are out in the open like this. It was Prescott who suggested that we use mental telepathy to discuss anything that we need to keep to ourselves.*"

"*Do you think that I am a Light Bearer like you?*" asked Hailey.

"*I believe so,*" said Lucas.

"*What is a Light Bearer supposed to do?*" asked Hailey.

"*My grandpa told me that a Light Bearer is someone with virtue and love who has the courage to make correct choices. He is to make his life a beacon of light for others. It has something to do with using light to drive away the darkness,*" answered Lucas.

Hailey thought about what she had just heard and said, "*I would think that a Light Bearer is someone who chooses to do the right thing even when no one is watching.*"

"*Wow!*" said Lucas, "*That is exactly what Katrina told me.*"

"So what did the vultures do?" asked Hailey. Lucas realized that he just had a brief thought about the vultures near his grandpa's home which prompted Hailey's question.

"When I was with my grandpa, we saw a dark cloud coming toward us. There was a bunch of vultures sitting on a fence nearby, and they flew right into the dark cloud and it disappeared. Prescott is always talking about lessons I need to learn. I think that was a lesson about driving away the darkness," said Lucas.

"Is there anything that we need to do as Light Bearers?" asked Hailey.

"You sure ask a lot of questions," said Lucas.

"I ask a lot of questions because that is how I learn and why I am so smart," replied Hailey with a grin.

Before Lucas could respond, they heard Hailey's mom call everyone to come and eat. Lucas released the hold on the ring and said, "We'll talk more about this later."

During dinner, the families were discussing different activities that each family enjoyed when both fathers discovered they enjoyed riding motorcycles in the desert. Andrew, Lucas's dad, said that every fall the family camps out in the desert not far from Barstow. He said that on the next trip he wanted to go to a ghost town and a turquoise mine, and invited Hailey's family to join them. Hailey's parents accepted the invitation and the dads started making plans right then. Lucas looked over at Hailey and even without the advantage of reading each others thoughts, both thought the idea of desert camping was cool.

After dinner, Lucas and Hailey went back outside and sat by the pool again. The school was behind Hailey's house, and Lucas thought he saw something strange in the trees on the school property along the fence line.

"Hailey," said Lucas, "turn around slowly and look at the trees near the corner of the fence and tell me what you see."

Hailey turned and looked at the trees.

"The leaves in one area are darker and look like the wavy lines you see in the road on a hot day," replied Hailey.

"That's what I see, too. It is about the size of a big umbrella," said Lucas.

"What do you think it is?" asked Hailey.

"I don't know, but it reminds me of the dark cloud I saw with my grandpa. Let me ask Prescott," said Lucas.

"Did you bring Prescott to our house?" asked Hailey,

"No. But because I have the Power Ring, he can hear my thoughts," said Lucas, as he turned the pointer to the symbol for mental telepathy.

"*Prescott. Can you help?*" asked Lucas.

"*What is it, Lucas?*" answered Prescott.

"*I don't know, but I see a strange shape in the trees behind Hailey's house,*" said Lucas. "*I was wondering if it was like the dark cloud that Grandpa and I saw on the walk over to Aunt Sophie's house.*"

"*I see it, too. It is indeed the same dark force you saw with Grandpa Jack.*" replied Prescott.

"*How do you see it? Are you here?*" asked Lucas.

"*No, I am not. But because of our mental connection, I can see what you see,*" said Prescott.

"*What should I do?*" asked Lucas.

Prescott wanted Lucas to learn to figure out problems on his own as much as possible. That was the best way for him to learn to overcome challenges in his life.

"*What do YOU think you should do?*" asked Prescott.

Sometimes Lucas got a little annoyed with Prescott's answers when he asked for help. But then Lucas realized that this was all part of the training process.

"*Is there another power on the ring that you can use?*" asked Hailey. Lucas had forgotten that she could also hear the mental conversation between himself and Prescott.

"*Excellent question, Hailey,*" replied Prescott. "*It is so nice to finally get to talk with you.*"

"*And it is exciting to talk with you as well,*" said Hailey. "*Lucas has told me so much about you. Okay, Lucas, you have the Power Ring. What are you going to do?*"

Lucas thought about the three powers available to him to get rid of the dark cloud.

Stopping time was probably not the solution. Maybe he could be invisible but that wouldn't help Hailey. Lucas tried to think of some way to use his mind.

Prescott then said, *"Lucas, you are already invisible to that dark force, but Hailey is not. Maybe it remembers seeing you and Hailey together at school, and it is hanging around Hailey to find you. Consider the elements around you. Determine what is available to remove the darkness."*

At first, Hailey was not frightened because she had seen what Lucas could do with the Power Ring. But she had no clue as to what happened to Lucas at his grandpa's house. Now that she heard a dark force was hanging around her to get to Lucas, she was starting to get a little concerned.

"Lucas," said Hailey very slowly. "You are going to do something, aren't you?"

Lucas thought about what Prescott had said about the elements. *"What are the elements around me?"* he asked himself.

"That's easy," said Hailey. *"The four elements are earth, water, air and fire."*

"But which element do I use?" asked Lucas.

"I don't know which one to use, but you had better decide quickly. That dark shape in the trees is either getting larger or it is getting closer," exclaimed Hailey.

The cloud was indeed getting closer as Hailey feared. They both stood and started backing up. Lucas quickly rotated the pointer to the three arrows, the symbol for telekinesis, and squeezed very hard. Lucas decided to use the element of water. He imagined a huge fire hose sucking up water out of the pool next to them and directing the blast at the dark cloud. The explosion of water from the cannon Lucas had created with his mind stripped away the cloud, and what remained was an image that Lucas and Hailey would not soon forget. It was about four feet tall with a deformed head and body with tiny arms and legs. It wasn't human or like any animal they had ever seen. Its eyes were red, and the angry face just added to the deformity of its head. Lucas and Hailey heard it scream in anger and it quickly retreated toward the school.

"What was that, Lucas?" asked a very frightened Hailey.

"I don't know," replied Lucas, who was shaking and trying to hide his own fears.

"That, my young friends," said Prescott, "was Rebulus the Light Thief. You have successfully removed him from your presence, but he is not going to quit easily. Remember, it is hard to beat someone that never gives up, and you must never give up. Never give up, never give in and you will win."

"What should we do?" asked Lucas. "You said that I was invisible to Rebulus but Hailey was not. Is there a way we can protect her too?"

"Yes there is. Are you alone and away from everyone else?" asked Prescott.

"We are on the side of my house by the pool, and everyone else is inside," replied Hailey.

"Very good," said Prescott, "now listen carefully. I think that you both need to know about Rebulus and to remember that he will try to harm you. Lucas, I put a protective shield on you at your grandfather's house and you can now do that for

Hailey. This will work because of our connection. Turn the pointer on the Power Ring to the sun symbol. Hold Hailey's hand in yours, and put the Power Ring between your hands and hold tight."

Lucas did exactly as Prescott instructed.

They then heard Prescott say, *"Alina koruma, alina koruma, alina koruma."*

Light started expanding from the Power Ring in their hands until Lucas and Hailey were both encircled in a ball of light. They felt like they were floating on a warm breeze. They heard the sound of rushing water. This might have gone on for several minutes, but they lost track of time. The light started to fade and retreat back into the Power Ring in their hands. They looked at each other and just smiled.

"I need to sit down. I feel light-headed," said Hailey.

It was only a few minutes after sitting down when Lucas's mother came around the corner of the house. "Lucas, it's time to go home," said his mom. She looked at all of the water on the patio around the pool. "Looks like you two were having some fun splashing all that water out of the pool."

Lucas and Hailey looked at each other and just smiled.

"Okay, Mom," said Lucas. He then turned to Hailey and said, "Thanks for having us over for dinner."

"Thank you for the adventure and the protection," replied Hailey as she winked at Lucas. "I guess we will talk later."

SEVEN

CAMPING WITH BEARS

Common sense is so rare it should be classified as a super power.

Lucas's parents, Andrew and Hannah, were planning a camping adventure for the family and decided to go to Yosemite National Park. When they arrived in the Yosemite Valley, Lucas was amazed by the beauty of the nature he saw around him.

Lucas said, "There's Half Dome. That's easy to spot from the pictures. What are some of the other places around the valley?"

His dad pointed out El Capitan, Yosemite Falls, Vernal Falls, and Glacier Point.

Lucas's mom said, "I have some old pictures in an album from Grandma Ellie that shows the famous 'fire falls' from Glacier Point. The people that owned the hotel on the top would build a large fire every night and then push red hot embers over the edge and onto the rocks below. At night it looked like a red fiery waterfall."

Lucas thought back to the fire at the school, but just before he started feeling the fear he usually felt, he remembered what Prescott had told him. Lucas looked up, smiled and thought about how strong he was. He then heard Prescott in his mind.

"That is good. I see that you are remembering to be in control of your thoughts," said Prescott.

Lucas just smiled and thanked Prescott in his mind. Lucas had left Prescott with his cousin, but Lucas was always able to talk with him in his mind.

Prescott then said, *"Lucas, you will need to be watchful of your family to keep them safe."*

"I will," said Lucas. His thoughts were interrupted by his brother Gavin.

"Can we see the fire falls tonight?" asked Gavin.

"Oh, no," replied Mom. "They ended the fire falls when Grandpa Jack was still in high school although he told me that he was able to see it when he was a kid."

The family got back in the car and headed up to a campground in the Yosemite high country.

"Where are we going to camp?" asked Lucas.

"We are going to the White Wolf Campground," replied Dad.

"Are there wolves there?" asked Gavin excitedly.

"There are no wolves," said Mom. "But we may see deer, mountain lions and bears. We will probably see squirrels and chipmunks, too."

Lucas's dad wasn't too concerned as he had read that the bears are usually timid and are just looking for food. The park ranger had told them that their food had to be stored in the food lockers at each campsite and never in the tent. The ranger said that they should all just use common sense when dealing with the animals, and they would not bother them.

The family arrived at White Wolf Campground and set up the tent near a small creek. Lucas and Gavin helped to put all of the food in the food locker. That afternoon, after they had the tent set up, the family walked down to the lake next to the campground. Lucas's dad told the kids to be on the lookout for any animals or birds and try to identify them. Lucas had brought Kevin's dog,

Ranger, on the trip. Ranger was always on a leash, but Lucas was not worried about him running away. Lucas and Ranger had talked before the trip, and Ranger agreed to be a good dog and to stay by Lucas.

As they neared the lake, Lucas said, "I see four deer on the other side of the lake and a hawk flying above us."

As they got closer, the deer looked up and stood very still. Lucas wondered if he would be able to talk with the deer. After Prescott's warning, Lucas always carried the Power Ring with him. With his mind, he turned the pointer to the symbol for mental telepathy and looked directly at the largest deer.

"Hi. My name is Lucas and my family is here to enjoy this beautiful place where you live. We are not here to hurt you."

The largest deer looked at the other deer and back to Lucas. In Lucas's mind he heard the deer say, *"I see that you have a special gift to talk with us. We are not frightened by people because we are able to run faster than you. All we ask is that you be kind to all the animals in the forest and keep your dog with you.*"

Lucas broke into the biggest smile and wished he could share what he had just heard with his family. Prescott had told him he would be able to tell his family soon, but not yet.

Lucas's little brother and sister went down to the lake and were skipping stones on the water with Dad. Ranger and Lucas lay down on a large rock, and Lucas looked up in the sky at a circling Red-Tailed Hawk and wondered if the hawk would hear him also.

"*Hello, Hawk. My name is Lucas. Can you hear me?*" asked Lucas.

"*I hear you, Lucas. I am called Kestrel. I can sense that you are a very special young man. Are you a Light Bearer?*" asked the hawk.

"*I am,*" replied Lucas. "*What do you know about Light Bearers?*"

"*I know that a Light Bearer can be trusted. If you need my help while you are here, I am at your service,*" replied the hawk.

Lucas thought back to the night of the barbeque at Hailey's house and remembered that Prescott could see what he saw and wondered if he could do that with the hawk.

Lucas asked the hawk, "*Kestrel, is it possible for me to see what you see?*"

"*All you need to do is to close your eyes and ask,*" replied the hawk.

Lucas closed his eyes and asked the hawk, "*May I see through your eyes?*"

Immediately, Lucas had what he could only describe as a fantastic vision, as he saw the world through the hawk's eyes. As Kestrel circled in the sky, Lucas saw his family by the lake, the deer, and he even saw himself lying on the rock next to Ranger. Lucas was amazed at hawk's clear vision as he saw the world in precise detail. He saw the pine needles on the trees, the sparkling flecks of black and gold in the granite rocks, several mice running through the grass and even the fish swimming in the lake.

Lucas said to the hawk, "*This is amazing! You have such wonderful vision.*"

Kestrel replied, *"I do indeed have a great gift of vision. But you are a human, and you too have a gift of vision. You can see things in your mind that do not exist and create them and make them visible. You have the ability to see the future that you want and shape that vision however you choose."*

Lucas began to realize that even this Red-Tailed Hawk had a lesson to teach him.

"What type food do you eat?" asked Lucas.

"I prefer rabbits, ground squirrels, and reptiles," replied the hawk. *"And sometimes I will feast on annoying birds like those jays in your camp ground."*

Lucas was enjoying the hawk's view of world when he saw that Kestrel had spotted a snake on the ground behind the rock where he was lying.

The hawk said, *"See that snake on the ground behind you? He will become food for me and my family. Remain still and watch."*

Lucas was able to see what the hawk saw as it started a dive and flew straight down for the snake. Lucas's mom was taking pictures while the others played. She was unaware of the hawk as she focused her camera and zoomed in on Lucas who appeared to be napping on the rock. Just as she snapped the picture, Ranger lifted his head and the hawk flew into the view finder swooping down with its talons outstretched.

She snapped another picture of the hawk on the ground behind Lucas and then another as the hawk beat its powerful wings and climbed into the sky with the snake.

Lucas's mom called to everyone. "Look at the hawk with the snake above Lucas!"

They all turned around to see the hawk flying over Lucas with the snake grasped firmly in its sharp talons. Lucas's mom ran over to wake Lucas and tell him what he had just missed.

"Lucas!" she said excitedly. "Did you see the hawk? There was a snake on the ground behind you and a hawk swooped down, grabbed the snake and flew off. It was fantastic! You should have seen it!"

"Too bad I missed it," said Lucas.

"I took some pictures so you can see what happened," assured his mom.

☘ ☘ ☘

That night at their campfire, Lucas's dad told a story about a magical dragon and of knights in a faraway kingdom. Lucas's little brother and sister fell asleep in their chairs listening to the story and mom and dad carried them to their sleeping bags inside the tent.

Lucas sat alone by the fire moving the coals around with a long stick as he listened to the sounds of the forest. He heard an owl in a nearby tree and what he thought was a coyote barking and then howling in the distance. He also heard the sound of frogs croaking from the creek in what sounded like a burping contest between kids at school.

When his dad returned, Lucas asked, "What is that crackling sound coming from the creek?"

Lucas's dad listened very intently until he heard it. "It sounds like twigs or branches breaking. The sound is getting louder like someone or something is walking in our direction."

As the crackling sound got closer, Ranger jumped up and started sniffing the air.

"What is it, Ranger?" asked Lucas.

Ranger cocked his head, raised his ears and replied to Lucas, *"It is a bear. It is coming this way. Do you want me to bark and scare it away?"*

"No." said Lucas.

"No what?" asked his dad,

"I was just telling Ranger not to bark," said Lucas, "I think it might be a bear coming this way."

"Why don't you get on the other side of the fire," said his dad as he threw two more logs onto the fire and grabbed the burning stick that Lucas had in the coals.

"Dad," said Lucas, "I think the bear is going to be more afraid of us than we are him."

"You are probably right," said his dad as he made sure the stick in his hand had a flame on the other end.

The sound continued to get louder as it approached their camp. Lucas's dad pointed his flashlight in the direction of the sound. The eyes of the bear glowed in the reflection of the flashlight as it lumbered to the edge of their camp and just sat down. Moments later, another bear wandered up to the edge of the camp and he too sat down. Ranger started to get a little anxious but remained next to Lucas, ready to protect him with his life.

"This is the strangest thing I have ever seen," said Lucas's dad nervously as a third bear arrived and sat near the other two bears.

Lucas had heard a lot of scary stories about bears, but he had a clear impression that these bears had a peaceful purpose for being there. He positioned the Power Ring to talk to the bears with his thoughts.

"Hello, Bear. My name is Lucas. Why are you here?"

The first bear replied, "Hello Lucas. I am called Thorben. A stranger has come to our forest, and she means to harm you. We are here to protect you and your family."

"How do you know? Who told you?" asked Lucas.

"No one told us. We just know," replied Thorben. "We will not bother you or your family. We will stay here at the edge of your camp until morning so you can sleep safely." The bears then turned around, faced toward the creek and sat down again.

"Dad," said Lucas, "I don't think the bears mean us any harm. It looks as if they might be guarding our camp."

"It certainly looks that way," said his dad, "but this is really strange behavior for wild bears."

Lucas and his dad talked quietly by the fire for some time while Lucas stirred the coals with his stick again. They continued to watch the silhouette of the

three bears and put more wood on the fire to push
the darkness back into the forest.

They talked about sports, bicycles, Prescott,
Hailey, school, cousins, Grandma Ellie and many
other things while watching the bears. The bears did
not move for over an hour from the spot where
they had settled.

It was getting late when Lucas's dad finally
said, "It looks like we might be watched over all

night by these gentle bears. We are certainly going to have a story to tell your mother in the morning."

With the fire nearly out, Lucas and his dad decided it was about time to leave the warmth of the fire for the warmth of their sleeping bags. Lucas's dad stood up and headed for the tent.

"I'm going to put a few more logs on the fire and I'll be along in a few minutes," said Lucas.

EIGHT

THE SHADOW WOLF

There is always a way if you are committed.

Lucas was sitting by the fire, and a young woman came out of the shadows of the forest and sat on the other side of the fire from him. She was pretty with a slender build, and Lucas guessed that she was maybe twenty years old. She was wearing a dark gray shirt, black pants and black boots. Her black hair covered her shoulders and hid part of her face. There was a white streak in her hair that fell down to her shoulders. The only color on her was her golden eyes as they reflected the yellow flames of the campfire. She was not wearing a jacket and she looked cold.

Lucas asked, "Do you want to warm yourself by the fire?"

She just nodded with a slight smile and said, "Yes, thank you," as she held up her hands to soak up the heat from the flames.

"My name is Lucas. What's your name?" asked Lucas.

She replied, "I am Senka."

Lucas noticed she had an accent. "That's a pretty name. I've never heard it before. Where are you from?" asked Lucas.

"I am from a different forest," replied the young woman.

"What does Senka mean?" asked Lucas.

"Darkness," she said, almost in a whisper.

Lucas saw Gavin come out of the tent and walk over to Senka. She put her arm around Gavin and gave him a hug and kissed his forehead like she was part of the family.

Senka then turned to Lucas and said, "Let's make a trade. I will trade Gavin for the Fire Crystal and your light."

Lucas's heart started pounding and almost responded in agreement to the trade. Then he remembered that Prescott had warned him to never begin a conversation with a dark force which he had just done. It was becoming clear that she was the type of darkness that Prescott had warned him about. Without any forethought for his own safety, Lucas rushed to grab Gavin and pull him away from

Senka, but Gavin disappeared, and Lucas was thrown into the fire. All of his fears of burning in a fire flooded back to his memory. That's when Lucas woke up shaking. He got up and peeked out of the tent to see the faint red glow of the fire. In the moonlight, he saw the outline of the bears still watching over the family so he crawled back into his sleeping bag and struggled to get back to sleep.

🐻 🐻 🐻

The next morning, Lucas's dad was the first to awake as the sky was turning a light gray. He stuck his head out of the tent and saw that the bears were gone. He walked over to where the bears had settled down and saw that the grass had been matted down. This confirmed what he remembered from last night, that the bears coming to their campsite really did happen.

When Lucas came out of the tent, his dad said, "As hard as it is to believe, I guess the bears really were guarding the camp. Rather than scare the rest of the family, let's not say anything and see what happens tonight."

After breakfast, the family drove down to the valley floor to go on a hike up the Mist Trail to Vernal Falls.

Lucas's mom said, "We need to be careful on the hike today. I read that there is a lot of water coming over the falls this year and the mist will make the trail slippery."

Lucas's little sister, Madison, was the princess in the family, but when she needed to, she would do her best to keep up with her brothers. Gavin and Madison took turns being the leader but always looked back to make sure that the rest of the family was still close. Lucas was thoroughly enjoying the hike up to Vernal Falls. Mom had said that there were over six hundred granite steps to the top of the falls, but Lucas lost count somewhere after two hundred steps. The mist from the waterfall created a cool breeze that kept Lucas from getting too hot.

Lucas had been thinking about Prescott's comment. He slowed down and dropped back on the trail about thirty feet behind his family.

"Prescott, will you explain what you meant when you said I needed to be watchful of my family and to keep them safe?" asked Lucas.

Prescott replied, "I may have underestimated the determination of Rebulus to get to you. The dream that you had last night suggests that he has enlisted the help of someone else. You met Senka in your dream, and you will probably meet her again. You need to be watchful. If needed, you too can enlist the help of others."

Lucas had a strong impression that he should catch up to Gavin, so he and Ranger started to run up the trail. Lucas saw Gavin walking ahead of the family, and there was a young woman walking on the trail beside him. She had long black hair, a gray shirt with black pants and black boots.

Lucas unhooked the leash on Ranger and said, "Ranger, run up the hill and start barking at the woman next to Gavin, but don't touch her."

Without questioning, Ranger sprinted toward the woman, past Madison and Lucas's parents, and was by Gavin's side in just a few seconds. Ranger got between Gavin and the young woman in black and continued to bark at her until Lucas's dad grabbed Ranger by the collar and pulled him back.

"I'm so sorry. I don't know what got into him," said Lucas's dad to the young woman.

"That's okay," she replied. "Sometimes animals have a mind of their own and will do dangerous things."

As Lucas came running up with the leash, the young woman in black turned to go back down the trail from where she had just come. She looked directly at Lucas and he recognized the flash of her golden eyes from his dream. She gave him a sly smile. As she walked by she leaned toward Lucas and whispered, "Maybe we will meet again."

"Dad," said Lucas, "I think there was something very bad about that lady in black. Why else would Ranger have barked at her the way he did? I think we need to stay closer together for the rest of the hike."

"That's fine with me," replied Lucas's father.

Lucas and his family finished their hike to the top of Vernal Falls. After a short rest for lunch, they headed back down the Mist Trail. Lucas decided to go first to make sure that no one in his family met up with Senka before he did.

Late that night, when Lucas and his father were the last ones sitting by the fire, the bears reappeared and took up their watch just as they had the night before.

"Lucas, I've been thinking about some of the changes over the past few months. There have been some strange events since you found Prescott," said Lucas's dad.

"What do you mean?" asked Lucas.

"Well, for starters, why are these bears camping out with us each night? Doesn't it seem just a little odd?" his father gently asked.

"I suppose so," replied Lucas. "But if they really are here guarding us, don't you feel a little safer?"

"I'm not so sure of that," replied his father. "Your mother and I have noticed that since you've had the responsibility to care for Prescott, you are acting lot more grown up. That's a good change."

Lucas replied, "I know that Prescott is just a chameleon, but he seems more like an old friend.

Sometimes I will talk to him and I imagine that he is talking back to me. He gives me advice, he gives me ideas and he helps me figure things out."

"What about the lady that gave Prescott to you? She was at that house one day and a few days later, it was as if she didn't exist. She did say that Prescott might be a magical chameleon. That might be the only way to explain all of the things that have happened since you found him," said his father.

Lucas did not want to say anything else that might give away the magical gift Prescott had given him, so he told his dad he was tired and wanted to go to sleep. He really was tired, but he didn't think he could sleep. He didn't want to have another dream like the one he had the night before.

Lucas was awakened by the sound of birds chirping as the eastern sky began to lighten. Lucas was the first one up this morning. As he stepped out of the tent, he saw that the bears were still at the edge of the camp. The three bears got up and started for the creek when largest bear turned to face Lucas.

"Lucas, we must go before the others awake. There is talk in the forest that you must avoid the wolf. If you require our help, we are here. Be careful my friend," said the bear.

"Thank you," replied Lucas. *"Thank you for watching over my family."*

ಙ ಙ ಙ

The next two days and nights of camping went by without any incidents, and Lucas began to relax. The three bears arrived late each night and were gone in the morning. On the last day, before they packed up, Lucas and Gavin asked if they could go fishing one more time at the lake near the campground. Lucas and Gavin were both good swimmers so their parents agreed they could fish, but only for an hour. The boys grabbed their poles and fishing tackle and ran to the lake. They cast their lines into the lake from the rocky shore but didn't get any nibbles from the fish there.

After a while, Gavin said, "I'm going over by the trees on the other side of the lake to see if the fish are biting there."

Lucas watched his brother walk around the lake. Gavin sat down on a large rock with his legs dangling over the edge. Gavin was several feet above the water and he thought this was a great spot to fish.

After a few minutes, Lucas hooked a fish and concentrated on reeling it in. The next time he looked up at Gavin, Lucas saw a gray wolf standing behind Gavin.

That's when he heard a voice in his head, *"Let's make a trade Lucas. I will trade you Gavin for the Fire Crystal and your light."*

Lucas's heart started racing as he remembered the dream. The dream did not end well so he tried to think of how he was going to get to Gavin before he was attacked by the wolf.

Lucas remembered that voice and looked behind the wolf to see if he could see Senka hiding in the trees. Lucas had been instructed to never begin a conversation in his mind with any dark force, so he just nodded in agreement at the wolf.

Lucas thought back to his conversation with Grandpa Jack about whether he was focusing on his fear or his courage. He most definitely needed to strengthen his courage right now. He knew that he needed to be smart and make sure the outcome was better than in his dream. Lucas put down his fishing pole and began walking slowly around the lake never taking his eyes off of Gavin or the wolf.

Gavin was unaware of anything going on behind him and continued fishing on the edge of the rock. As Lucas walked around to the other side of the lake, he formulated a possible rescue plan. With the Power Ring set, he called out to the bears.

"Thorben, can you help me?" asked Lucas, hoping he would hear him and arrive in time. He saw the hawk soaring overhead and asked for his help as well, not knowing what they would do.

As Lucas got closer, he kept glancing toward the trees expecting to see Senka hiding there. He looked at the wolf again and saw the unmistakable golden eyes and the white streak in the dark fur. Lucas realized that Senka was the wolf.

Lucas called out again to the bears, "*Bears. Can you help me?*"

Thorben replied, "*We are ready when you are. Just tell us when to move. We have called on some other friends that will be there when needed.*"

Lucas stopped about ten feet from the wolf.

He heard Senka's voice again, "*Put the Fire Crystal on the tree stump, and you and your brother can walk away.*"

Lucas remembered that Prescott had said. "*Never, ever, start a conversation with a dark force. They will speak nothing but lies of the blackest night.*"

Lucas did not believe that the wolf would let them walk away. Even though he was afraid, he knew he had to find the courage to fight. Lucas moved closer to the tree stump and reached into his pocket. When Lucas had set down his fishing pole, he had picked up a round flat stone about the size of the Power Ring. He pulled the stone from his pocket.

As he set the stone on the tree stump, he shouted, "*Now, my friends!*"

Lucas had set the Power Ring and used his telekinetic power. Before Gavin could turn around, using his mind, Lucas yanked the pole from Gavin's hands and sent him and the pole flying into the lake. At the same moment, eight or nine hawks came at the wolf from behind and began dropping jagged rocks from their talons onto the wolf's head and back.

The wolf was surprised and completely caught off guard thinking that Lucas was easy prey. Almost immediately, a swarm of bees descended on the wolf to sting her face and head. The bees must have been the other creatures the bears had called upon to help. Finally, six huge bears came crashing out of the trees and attacked the wolf. The sounds of the wolf yelping and the bears growling filled the forest as Lucas dove from the fishing rock into the water to rescue Gavin. As Lucas was helping his brother swim to the shore near their camp, he looked back and saw the wolf running up the canyon behind the lake.

Back at camp, Gavin excitedly told his parents about the huge fish that took the bait and pulled him and his pole into the lake. He was lucky that Lucas was there to help him swim to the shore.

The boys changed into dry clothes and helped pack up the tent and the other camping equipment. Before he got into the car to leave, Lucas looked up to see a lone hawk circling above the meadow.

Silently Lucas said, *"Thank you Kestrel for helping me today. Tell the others that I am grateful for their service."*

"*I will tell the others of your gratitude,*" replied the hawk.

Lucas then heard Thorben reply, "*Lucas Light Bearer, my friend, you are most welcome*"

NINE
NEW KID ON THE BLOCK

Our life is defined by the choices we make.

Lucas was really glad to be back in his own house, his own room and his own bed. He was glad to be home with Prescott. When Lucas's parents said they were planning a camping adventure, they had no idea how adventurous it was going to be.

Lucas had a lot of questions on his mind that he hoped Prescott would answer. Lucas got Prescott from his cousin and put the cage back on the desk in his room.

"Prescott," asked Lucas, "Can you tell me who or what Senka is and why she was in Yosemite?"

Prescott replied, *"I said earlier that I may have underestimated the determination of Rebulus. He recruited Senka to take the ring from you. Without the Power Ring, you lose the ability to protect yourself and others. To answer your question, Senka is a woman that has the ability to let you see what she wants you to see. She can take the form of the young woman you saw on the trail or of the wolf you saw by the lake. She is evil, no matter what form she takes."*

"What's to prevent her from finding me or my family here?" asked Lucas.

"Nothing," replied Prescott. *"There are many like Rebulus and Senka. The names and the faces may change, but their intent is the same. They do not want you to be a Light Bearer."*

"How can I protect my family and friends with the darkness always after me?" asked Lucas.

"Lucas, I want you to stand up and look in the mirror and tell me what you see," said Prescott. Lucas stood up, looked in the mirror and said, "I see myself."

"Can you describe what you see?" asked Prescott.

"I see a ten-year-old boy with blondish-brown hair wearing a blue t-shirt and brown shorts. He has a scar below his chin from a fall on the cement steps," said Lucas.

"*What else do you see Lucas?*" asked Prescott.

This was really hard for Lucas. Sure, he looked in the mirror every day, but he never really thought much about who was looking back.

"Okay," said Lucas, "I see Lucas Andrew Lightfoot, the oldest son of my parents and the big brother to Gavin and Madison. I see gray-blue eyes looking back at an ordinary boy."

"*Lucas, you are anything but ordinary. In fact, you are extraordinary,*" replied Prescott.

"Okay Prescott, what do you see when you look at me?" asked Lucas.

"*I will tell you what I see,*" said Prescott. "*I see everything you just said, but I see more. I see someone with a desire to do the right thing. I see someone who is kind to the weak and someone who is true to his family and friends. I see someone who is a leader among his friends who lets his light shine so that others will be influenced for good. I see someone with light in his eyes.*"

"How do you see all of that?" asked Lucas. "Can you see the future?"

"*No, I cannot see the future,*" answered Prescott. "*But I know that we each create our own future by our choices and actions. We are defined by the choices we make.*"

Prescott was quiet for a moment so the impact of what he said could sink into Lucas's mind.

"*When you look in the mirror,*" continued Prescott, "*you see a mask of who you think you are today. As you take off that mask, you see a mask of who you could become. Take that one off, and you can see who you truly are, a Light Bearer.*"

Lucas was not too sure about what mask he was wearing, but if Prescott could see through to who he really was, then maybe he needed to see himself as Prescott did.

"*Lucas,*" said Prescott, "*I am very pleased with your actions during your camping trip. I told you before, the more you use the Power Ring, the more you will know what to do. You listened to the animals and they became your friends and helped you. Your dream was a gift to you to help prepare you for what was to come. When you needed to save Gavin, you did not think about your own safety. But, you were smart and considered the options available to you.*"

"I remembered Grandpa telling me to be brave and be smart when faced with a dark force like this," said Lucas.

"*You did the right thing by using your mind to look at the problem and search for solutions. The other smart thing you did was to ask for help. You need to remember that there are people, and animals, all around you that are willing to help. All you need to do is ask. You listened to your heart and followed the inspiration,"* said Prescott.

"Was this part of my test?" asked Lucas.

"You will be tested everyday in some way. Some are small tests and others will be big trials. Some are so big that you will wonder if you can be victorious. Each one will lead you to examine your life to see if your light is shining," replied Prescott.

ℊ ℊ ℊ

The house across the street was for sale and had been vacant for the last two months. Before they went camping, Lucas noticed that the "For Sale" sign in front of the house now had a "SOLD" sign and Lucas wondered who was going to be moving in. Several days after returning home, Lucas saw a huge moving truck on the street blocking the view of the house.

"Lucas," called his mom, "do you want to go with us to take these cookies to our new neighbors and welcome them to the neighborhood?"

Lucas's mom had baked a large batch of cookies, and once the moving truck was gone, Lucas and his family went to introduce themselves. Lucas learned that there were two children, both girls, in the Fontaine family. The oldest girl was fourteen and the younger one was Lucas's age. Her name was Mallory. She was just a little shorter than Lucas and had long brown hair. Mallory seemed excited about everything and was always moving her hands when she talked. She reminded Lucas of a little elf and wondered if she had little pointed ears under her hair. Lucas learned that her father's employer had transferred him from Texas, which explained the Southern accent. Lucas found that Mallory was very easy to talk to and liked her at once.

Mallory asked, "Lucas, what school do you go to?"

Lucas told her a little about the school and where it was.

Lucas added, "There was a fire at the school about a month ago, but they say that the repairs will be made before school starts in the fall." He didn't say anything about rescuing Anna during the fire.

"This will be the first time I am attending a public school," said Mallory. "My mom has always home-schooled us, but she is going to work now."

Mallory asked lots of questions and seemed to be sincerely interested in Lucas and his family.

"You are a lot like my friend Hailey," said Lucas. "You both ask a lot of questions."

"I hope that's a good thing," said Mallory. "I would like to meet your friend."

The more they talked, the more Lucas thought how smart she was. She seemed to know a lot of stuff about many things, and he figured, like Hailey, she had a very curious mind.

The next day, Lucas invited Hailey over to the house so she could meet Mallory. Lucas and Hailey were in the back yard where he was telling Hailey about some of the adventures on their camping trip. He was just getting to the part about fishing on the last day when he heard the door bell ring, and Mallory came out into the back yard. Lucas introduced the girls to each other and they all sat on the trampoline and talked for almost an hour about many things. Lucas did not say anything about Prescott, and Hailey picked up on that and kept quiet about Prescott as well. As they were sitting on the trampoline, a bright green bird with a red head landed on a branch in the tree just a few feet away from them.

"Look at that beautiful bird," exclaimed Mallory. "What is it?"

"That's a Red-Crowned Parrot," said Lucas. "There are actually a lot of wild parrots is this area."

Just then, a second parrot landed on the branch next to the first. Hailey was surprised that the parrots were so close to them and seemed to be unafraid. She noticed that the parrots were making a very quiet chirping sound and she had the impression that they were whispering to each other.

"Where do they come from?" asked Mallory.

"I'm not sure. Do you know about the parrots, Hailey?" asked Lucas.

Hailey replied, "One story that I heard is that somebody had a lot of parrots in their home. When the house caught on fire, the owner let them all escape to save them, and they've been living in the wild ever since. There are now thousands of parrots living in the area."

"That is so cool," said Mallory. "I would never have imagined that parrots from the jungle would be living in the wild in our neighborhood." Mallory looked at the parrot and asked, "Polly want a cracker?"

Lucas, Hailey and Mallory all laughed. The parrots looked at the trio, squawked loudly and flew away.

After Mallory went home, Hailey said, "There is something about Mallory that I don't like."

"What do you mean?" asked Lucas feeling very defensive.

"I don't know. There's just something about her that doesn't seem right. It's almost like she's showing us what she wants us to see. It's like she's wearing a mask and hiding who she really is," said Hailey.

"I think you're jealous that there's another pretty girl at our school," said Lucas. "I think she's very nice, and I don't think she's hiding anything."

"It has nothing to do with jealousy," declared Hailey. "I think that there is more to her than what she is telling us."

This was the first time that Lucas and Hailey had argued. It didn't feel good, but Lucas thought he was right about Mallory. Hailey said that she needed to go home and hopped off the trampoline and left by the side gate.

Lucas went into his room and heard Prescott ask, *"Hailey does not think much of Mallory, does she?"*

"Hailey is just jealous that a pretty girl has moved across the street from me," replied Lucas.

"If it is just jealousy, I would not worry. Hailey will get over it. If it is something more, I would caution you to listen to your heart and maybe listen to Hailey," suggested Prescott.

Lucas took the Power Ring out of his pocket and placed it in the box he had retrieved from the cavity under the bridge. He had hidden the box under the bottom drawer in his dresser. He wanted to be alone without Prescott listening in on his thoughts. Lucas got the leash from the garage and told his mom that he was going to take Ranger for a walk and go over to his cousin's house. She said okay, but to be home in time for dinner.

Out on the sidewalk, Lucas said, "Ranger, it must be great being a dog. You don't have to worry about girls or lizards."

Lucas waited for a response and then realized that he did not have the Power Ring with him, and

Ranger could not hear his thoughts. Ranger seemed to be extremely agitated as he looked up and down the street. Ranger then pulled on the leash as he pawed the ground trying to move in the direction of Mallory's house. Lucas saw some people inside a car in front of Mallory's house, and then he saw Mallory run out of the house to get into the car. Ranger started barking and kept pulling Lucas's arm with the leash.

"Ranger! Stop that!" commanded Lucas. "That's my friend Mallory."

Mallory saw Lucas and waved, calling out to him, "Thanks for introducing me to Hailey. She's a really nice girl. I think that we will be good friends."

"Where are you going," asked Lucas.

Mallory replied, "We're taking my aunt to the airport. See you later."

Lucas waved to Mallory and turned to walk down to the foot bridge near Kevin's house, but he had to pull hard on the leash to get Ranger to follow him.

Mallory got in the back seat next to her aunt and gave her hand a squeeze. The car drove down the street away from the direction that Lucas was walking.

"It was so nice to visit with you, Aunt Senka," said Mallory. "I hope you can visit longer the next time."

"I hope so, too, Mallory. I hope so too," said Senka as she turned to look out the back window at Lucas.

TEN

ONE MORE SENSE

It is not what we get but who we become that gives meaning to our lives.

Lucas was sitting at the kitchen table staring into his bowl of cereal when his mom walked in and interrupted his thoughts about Hailey and Mallory.

"What's wrong, Lucas?" asked his mom. "You've been moping around the house for the past week. Is something bothering you?"

Lucas hesitated, and then said, "Do you remember the day that Hailey and Mallory came over last week?"

"Sure, I do. The three of you sat on the trampoline talking. Why? Did something happen?" asked Lucas's mother.

"After Mallory left, Hailey told me that she did not like her and thought that Mallory was hiding something," said Lucas.

"That seems really strange that Hailey would say something as bold as that about someone she just met," said Mom.

"That's exactly what I thought," replied Lucas. "I think that Hailey is jealous, and I told her so. That's when she got mad at me and went home."

"Lucas, there is something very special about Hailey. You and I both know that. There is a light in her eyes that is very unique," said Mom. "I know Hailey, but I do not know Mallory very well, and you should at least consider Hailey's feelings. She might be right."

"So you're against me, too!" exclaimed Lucas.

"Lucas, I am never against you,' said his mother. "There is something that you will learn as you get older. Many people have the ability or a power that is like a sixth sense where they can feel an impression about something or someone. I'm sure Hailey has that ability."

"What do you mean?" asked Lucas.

"People have five senses. With these senses, we gather information from the world around us. These senses are sight, sound, touch, taste and smell.

116

For some people, there is another sense that is a feeling. Some people feel it in their stomach and may say that they have a 'gut feeling,'" said Mom.

"Oh, yeah," said Lucas, "I've heard Dad say that he has a 'gut feeling' about something."

"That's right. Some people have a similar feeling in their heart or a thought in their mind," said Mom.

Lucas thought back to some of the experiences that he had had. The most vivid one was when he had the strong feeling that Gavin was in danger. He felt like he needed to run up the trail to Gavin and found Senka walking next to him.

"I think I understand," said Lucas. "When we were hiking on the trail up to the waterfall, I had a feeling that Gavin was in danger, and I told Ranger to go protect Gavin."

Mom was surprised and replied, "Does Ranger always do what you say?"

Lucas thought about how he should answer. Prescott had told him that his secret regarding the Power Ring was not to be shared with his family just yet, but soon.

Lucas just answered, "I think that Ranger sensed that there was something bad about the lady walking next to Gavin. That's when he ran up and started barking at her."

Lucas's mom sat down at the table next to Lucas and gave him a hug and said, "When you had a feeling you acted on it. We don't know if something bad would have happened to Gavin, but I am glad that you followed your feelings," said Mom.

Lucas's mom continued, "I think that the sixth sense is like a muscle. If we use a muscle, it gets stronger. If we act on and follow the feeling we have, then it gets stronger, and it becomes easier to recognize that we need to act."

Lucas remembered that Prescott had told him that the more he used the Power Ring for good, the more of a connection to the ring he would have. With the help of the Power Ring, ideas would come along with thoughts, feelings and impressions that would help Lucas make decisions.

Lucas had not held the Power Ring or talked with Prescott for over a week. He felt hurt that people were telling him that he might be wrong about Mallory. Lucas was beginning to realize that he felt alone without his friends, Prescott and Hailey.

"I think it would be good to call Hailey and ask her about the feeling she had about Mallory. Maybe she will explain why she felt that way," said Mom.

"Do you think that Hailey still likes me?" asked Lucas.

"I'm sure of it," replied Mom.

Lucas called Hailey later that day to see if they could talk. Hailey agreed and her mom dropped her off at Lucas's house on her way to the store. Hailey and Lucas went outside in the backyard, and Ranger came running over to them.

"I thought Kevin was going to take Ranger back when he came home from his dad's house in Las Vegas," said Hailey.

"He was," said Lucas, "but Kevin is staying with his dad for the school year, and he asked if I could keep Ranger for a while longer. My mom and dad said it was okay so Ranger is now our guard dog."

"What did you want to talk about," asked Hailey as they climbed on to the tire swing.

"My mom says that you might have a sixth sense about things and that I should listen to you," said Lucas. "Will you tell me why you don't like Mallory?"

"It's not that I don't like Mallory," Hailey said. "I hardly know her. But when we were sitting on the trampoline, I had a feeling that she was going to hurt you somehow."

"What do you mean?" asked Lucas.

"I was upset last week and bothered by some of the things you said. That night, I had a dream about you and Mallory," said Hailey.

"What was the dream about?" asked Lucas.

"You and Mallory were talking, and she may have hypnotized you," said Hailey. "Then Mallory said, 'I want you to meet someone.' Mallory disappeared and a woman came up behind you. She looked like Mallory but a little older, and she put her hands on your shoulders. This woman started pulling light out of you until you were very weak. Then she put you into a cage and dropped the cage into a lake or maybe it was a river. I saw you sink to the bottom."

"What happened?" asked Lucas.

"I don't know," replied Hailey. "I woke up."

Lucas then told Hailey about the dream he had with the woman at the campfire and about the wolf that spoke to him at the lake. He told her about all the animals in the forest and how they helped to fight off the wolf so he could get Gavin to safety.

"The wolf told me that she wanted to trade Gavin for the Power Ring and my light," said Lucas.

"Wait a minute," said Hailey. "You said that the wolf was a she and the woman had a white streak in her hair?"

"Yes. Why?" asked Lucas.

"Because Mallory's friend was a woman," said Hailey. "The woman you described in your dream was the same woman in my dream. She was wearing a gray shirt and black pants and boots. She was older than me and had black hair just the way you described her."

Lucas started getting goose bumps as he compared his dream to Hailey's dream. "Maybe you do have a sixth sense," said Lucas.

"From what you told me, I think you have a sixth sense, too, Lucas. It may be blocked somehow when you are around Mallory," said Hailey.

Lucas's mother stepped out of the back door to tell Hailey that her mother just called and would be there to pick her up in ten minutes. Lucas and Hailey walked into the house and were going to wait on the front porch for her mom when Hailey heard Prescott speak to her mind.

"Hailey, this is Prescott. Can we talk before you go?"

Before she could reply, everyone and everything in the house stopped moving except Hailey. She noticed that it became very quiet and she could not hear any sounds. She turned around to say something to Lucas and saw that he stood motionless.

"Hailey," said Prescott, *"I have something for you. Please come to Lucas's room."*

Hailey guessed that Prescott had stopped time for everyone except her. She left Lucas in the hallway and went to find Prescott. She walked by Gavin's room and saw Gavin, Madison and their mother kneeling around a puzzle on the floor. They too were frozen in time. She found Prescott in his cage in Lucas's room.

"*Hello, Hailey. It is nice to see you again,*" said Prescott.

"It's nice to see you, too, Prescott," said Hailey.

"*Hailey, I am concerned that Lucas may need some help,*" said Prescott.

"What do you mean? What can I do?" asked Hailey.

"*I feel the time will come soon when you will need to help Lucas,*" said Prescott, "*and I have something to help you. I want you to open the bottom drawer of Lucas's dresser and take the drawer out.*"

Hailey did as instructed by Prescott. She pulled the bottom drawer all the way out and let it fall to the floor.

"*Look under the dresser. Remove the box and open the lid,*" instructed Prescott.

Hailey reached under the dresser and found a square metal box and pulled it out. She set the golden box on the floor and opened the lid. Inside she saw the Power Ring that Lucas had used at her house.

"What do you want me to do?" asked Hailey.

"*Take the Power Ring and turn the pointer to the sun symbol and place the ring back into the box upside down and close the lid to the box,*" said Prescott.

Hailey did as Prescott instructed. Within a few seconds, Hailey heard a *click* sound coming from the box and saw a small compartment on the side of the box open up to reveal another Power Ring. It was golden in color with a blue crystal in the center. Hailey was surprised and exclaimed, "Oh, it's beautiful."

"Hailey, I want you to take this golden Power Ring with the blue water crystal, and I will instruct you on how to use it," said Prescott. *"There may come a time when you can use this ring to help Lucas. There may be a need of a second Light Bearer to rescue him. Please return the box the way that you found it."*

Hailey put everything back with the golden box under the dresser and closed the bottom drawer.

"What do I do now?" asked Hailey.

"*You do not need to do anything right now except keep the Power Ring safe. I will give you instruction when the time comes,*" replied Prescott. "*Lucas is unaware of the second ring. Do not tell anyone that you have the ring, including Lucas. There are some that would harm you and Lucas to get the ring. Now, it is time to go back to the hall where you were with Lucas. Your mother is here take to you home.*"

Hailey put the Power Ring in her pocket and rushed back to the hall. She was filled with excitement to be trusted with a Power Ring but she also felt some concern from the warning that Prescott gave her. She turned her back to Lucas and faced the front door like she was before time had been stopped. She heard the sounds increase but before she could take a step, Lucas ran right into the back of her.

"Hey! Why did you stop?" asked Lucas.

"I heard something," replied Hailey.

"Yeah, it was the doorbell," said Lucas.

Hailey opened the door and her mother asked, "Are you ready to go?"

"Sure," replied Hailey.

As she stepped onto the porch, Hailey turned around and said, "I am glad that we had this talk, Lucas. Thanks for listening to me."

Lucas just smiled and nodded and closed the front door.

As Hailey walked to the car, she heard Prescott speak in her mind.

"Hailey, I will be able to talk to your mind and explain how to use the ring as long as you have the ring in your possession. You do not have to keep it with you all of the time, but remember to always keep it safe. This power is to be treated with respect. The actions you take and who you become with this power will define who you are."

All the way home Hailey kept wondering what Prescott meant when he said that Lucas would need to be rescued. She decided that she would be on her guard and look out for Lucas, especially when Mallory was around.

ELEVEN

THIEF IN THE NIGHT

Never give in to despair and the dark will never triumph.

For the past week, Lucas had not used the Power Ring because he had been mad at Hailey and Prescott. He thought that they were wrong about Mallory. As his heart softened, Lucas decided that maybe he was more hurt than mad. Lucas knew that Prescott could talk to him anytime with or without the Power Ring and figured that Prescott was just giving him some time alone to think. After his talk with Hailey, Lucas was accepting the possibility that Hailey might indeed have a sixth sense. She might even be right about Mallory, but he wanted to give Mallory a chance to prove herself to be a friend.

Lucas gave Prescott some crickets and plopped down on his bed.

"Thank you, Lucas. I am glad to see that you are back," said Prescott.

"Hi, Prescott, I am sorry I've been upset," said Lucas.

"It is not unusual to feel hurt when others do not agree with you on something you believe. I think

that Mallory can be a friend, but I caution you not to share any information about the Power Ring," said Prescott.

"You know that I will not say anything to Mallory," assured Lucas.

"I know that you will not say anything intentionally, but you still need to be careful if you are alone with Mallory," cautioned Prescott.

℘ ℘ ℘

The day before the new school year started, the students and the parents were invited to an ice cream social hosted by the school and the Parent Teacher Association. This was so the new students could get a tour of the school and the way that the school notified the students which class they would be in and who their teachers would be. Lucas's mom invited Mallory and her mom to ride over to the school with them so they could get a tour of the school and show Mallory her classroom. Hailey arrived about ten minutes after Lucas and Mallory, and she saw them sitting at a table eating ice cream. Hailey decided to stay on the other side of the blacktop with another friend and just watch. Before long, Mr. Mason, the principal, came out of the office to welcome everyone to a new school year. He introduced two new teachers, Miss Miller and Mrs. Moore, and made a few comments about rebuilding the cafeteria and some of the classrooms after the fire.

Mr. Mason said, "The rosters for all of the students and their teachers have been posted on the wall. Go look for your name and then go to the classroom to meet your teacher."

"Come on, Mallory, let's find out who your teacher is," said Lucas.

Hailey watched them as they looked for their names, and she could hear Lucas when he said, "Mallory, we're in the same class."

"Oh great!" muttered Hailey under her breath.

Hailey watched Lucas, Mallory and their mothers head over to their classroom. Hailey went to the roster and saw that she, too, was in Miss Harrison's class with Lucas and Mallory, and thought that at least she could keep an eye on Mallory. Hailey did not need to see the classroom nor did she want to run into Lucas and Mallory today, so she headed home.

The next morning, Lucas was excited to see Hailey out in front of the school. As they walked to class, he said, "I didn't see you yesterday. Did you know we are in the same class?"

"Yes, I came by later and checked my class," said Hailey.

When they got to the classroom, Hailey saw that Mallory was already sitting at a desk. Mallory waved to Lucas and Hailey and motioned them to find a seat by her.

Lucas said, "Let's go sit by Mallory."

Hailey replied, "Okay." But inside she was thinking, *"There is no way I want to sit near Mallory, but I need to be near her to keep an eye on her."*

Miss Harrison said, "All right class. The bell has rung. Let's settle down. I want to welcome returning students and our three new students, Mallory, Brittney and Mabel."

Miss Harrison let the new girls tell a little about themselves and where they had lived before. Both Mabel and Brittney said that they had moved from Northern California near Sacramento, and Mallory was from Austin, Texas.

Miss Harrison said, "I volunteered to move up one grade so I know about half of you, but the rest of you are new to me. I am going to arrange you in alphabetical order by rows to help me remember your names. If you could all stand up and move to the sides of the room, you can sit back down in order when I call your name. We will start with Mabel in the first seat of row one."

Miss Harrison started calling out the names, and the students took their assigned seats. Hailey was concerned that she would not get to sit near Lucas. Mallory Fontaine was assigned a seat in the back of the second row and, Lucas was assigned a seat in row three next to Mallory.

"Oh, great," thought Hailey. "Mallory gets to be next to Lucas, and I will end up sitting in the front of the class."

As the names were called, Hailey was watching and hoping she would be next to Lucas. She was counting seats trying to figure out where she would be sitting. Kenny Scott's name was called to sit next to Lucas and Hailey's heart sank.

"Kenny, Kenny Scott?" asked Miss Harrison.

One of the kids who knew Kenny said that he had broken his leg when he crashed his bicycle in an accident and would miss the first few weeks of school.

"All right, the next name is Hailey Sinclair," said Miss Harrison. "Hailey, will you please take the seat next to Lucas Lightfoot?"

Although Hailey was not in the habit of wishing misfortune on anyone, she was happy that Kenny had broken his leg.

Lucas said, "This is great. We all get to sit together."

Hailey saw Mallory smile at her when she sat down, but Mallory's smile did not extend to her eyes, nor did it match the feeling she had about Mallory. Hailey decided that she was in the perfect seat to watch both Lucas and Mallory.

It had been two weeks since Prescott had given Hailey the golden Power Ring. He had instructed her how to use it for communicating with thought and how to be invisible. The symbols for those two powers were the same as on Lucas's Power Ring. There were three other symbols that were the same as Lucas's Power Ring. They were the symbols to stop time, telekinesis and the sun symbol. There were three other symbols that were different. Prescott told Hailey that the next power he would teach her was how to use the power of suggestion but he said that the other two powers were too dangerous to use at this time. Hailey had practiced being invisible and thought that would come in handy if Mallory ever got Lucas alone. She could be near them and neither of them would know she was there. Hailey knew that she could not say anything against Mallory, at least for now.

"Lucas," said Hailey in a whisper as she leaned closer, "Can we talk alone at lunch?"

"Sure," replied Lucas. "I brought my lunch. Let's go to the tables by the grass. What do you want to talk about?"

"Just some Prescott stuff," she said with a smile.

Lucas gave a nod knowing what she meant.

During the lunch period, Lucas and Hailey found a table where they could be alone, and Lucas asked, "What did you want to talk about?"

Hailey asked, "Do we still have our agreement that we can listen in on each other's thoughts?"

"Sure," replied Lucas. "Why do you ask?"

Hailey replied, "If you have the Power Ring with you while we are in class, we can talk and not disturb anyone."

"You mean we can talk and Mallory won't hear," said Lucas.

"Well, that, and Miss Harrison won't know either," replied Hailey. "Also, we won't get into trouble for talking."

"Okay, but we will have to end the permission anytime we are taking a test," said Lucas. "It wouldn't be honest if we shared answers."

"I agree, I don't think that a Light Bearer would want to cheat," said Hailey.

They both thought that it was nice to be back in school and talking as friends again.

ᔓ ᔓ ᔓ

Mr. Mason was planning the Back to School Night. For the opening assembly, he asked Lucas and his parents if they would come and bring his pet chameleon to the assembly. He wanted to publicly thank Lucas for saving Anna when he had gone back to the classroom to get Prescott. Lucas reluctantly agreed. He did not want to share too much information about Prescott nor did he want to be the center of attention.

While the family was at the school assembly, a dark figure walked along the creek behind Lucas's house. Ranger heard a noise and sniffed the air. He saw the shadow and recognized the scent immediately. Ranger began barking wildly at the stranger and ran from his dog house until the chain became tight and prevented him from reaching the intruder.

The stranger looked toward Ranger and said, "Silence!" Then it let out a low and menacing growl. Ranger whimpered and slinked back to his dog house. The stranger went straight to the window of Lucas's room, ripped off the screen, smashed the glass and easily jumped up and through the window. Moments later, the stranger dove out of the window, rolled on the lawn and leaped over the back fence to the creek.

Later that night, after the school assembly, Lucas walked into his room and felt the cold night air. When he turned on the light he saw why. The window was shattered and broken glass was all over his bedroom floor. Lucas set Prescott's cage on the desk and saw the golden box opened on the floor. His heart sank when he saw that it was empty.

"Mom, Dad, we've been robbed!" shouted Lucas.

TWELVE
SHERLOCK HAILEY

There are no mistakes. There are no failures. There are only lessons for us to learn.

By the time the police left, it was nearly midnight. They asked Lucas's dad to close the bedroom door and leave everything untouched until they could send some investigators the next day to look for clues. Nothing else was missing from the home and the police figured that the ring Lucas found in the back of the book must have some great value to someone. Lucas had an idea of who was behind the theft.

When he was alone with Prescott, Lucas asked, "Do you know who did this?"

"*Let me ask Ranger,*" replied Prescott. "*You may listen in on our conversation.*"

"*Ranger, this is Prescott. Do you know who broke into the house?*"

"*Yes I do. It was the woman Lucas saw on the trail,*" replied Ranger. "*She has a very different smell from other women. I know it was her. She smelled*

139

like a woman and a wolf. I barked to scare her away and I tried to go after her but the chain would not let me go very far. Then she growled at me and I got scared."

"Thank you," replied Prescott. "You did well. We know who is responsible."

Lucas slept on the couch that night and continued his conversation with Prescott in his mind.

"Prescott, how am I going to get the Power Ring back?" asked Lucas. *"How could I have done a better job at hiding it? How did she find it? Who do you think she is? I am so sorry I lost the ring. I made a terrible mistake!"*

"Lucas, slow down," replied Prescott. *"This is not your fault, and you did not make a mistake. This is only a lesson for you to learn."*

"I know. There are always lessons for me to learn," replied Lucas, almost in tears. *"What should I do?"*

"What you should do is go to sleep," replied Prescott. *"I will think about it tonight and see if I can come up with a solution tomorrow."*

It was late and Lucas was tired, but he had a million questions swirling around in his head. He finally drifted off to sleep about an hour after talking with Prescott. Lucas was asleep when Prescott reached out to Hailey in her dreams to tell her that Lucas needed help with an investigation and asked her to talk with Lucas at school.

The next day, Lucas stayed home in the morning to answer questions from the investigators. The only clue they found was some blood on a piece of glass that stuck out from the window frame. They concluded that the thief must have been cut climbing through the window. Both of the side gates had locks that were undisturbed. They found some footprints by the back fence and decided that the thief had climbed over from the creek.

Lucas did not get to school until lunchtime. "Lucas, what happened?" asked Hailey, "I heard that someone broke into your house last night."

"Wow, bad news really travels fast. How did you find out?" asked Lucas.

"Brittney told me. She heard it from Sarah, who was in the school office when your mom called the school to let them know you would be late. Do they know who did this?" asked Hailey.

"The police don't know, but I do," said Lucas. "It was the woman I met on the camping trip. She was the same woman that was in my dream. It was Senka."

"Are you sure," ask Hailey. "How do you know?"

Lucas asked, "Did you know that a dog's sense of smell is ten thousand times stronger than a human's sense of smell?"

"No, I didn't," replied Hailey. "What does that have to do with Senka?"

"Dogs have the ability to smell millions more smells than we can," said Lucas. "There is no doubt. Prescott asked Ranger if he knew who broke into our house, and Ranger was positive it was the same woman. And get this! Ranger said she smelled like a woman and a wolf."

"I think that is so cool that you can talk with an animal," said Hailey. "I wish I could do that."

"I can only do that now with Prescott since I lost the ring," said Lucas as his shoulders slumped.

"The Power Ring was stolen?" asked Hailey.

"Yes," replied Lucas. "Nothing else in the house was missing. My room was the only room the thief was in."

"Cheer up, Lucas," said Hailey. "I am sure you will get the Power Ring back. What can I do to help?"

"Prescott told me that when he could think of a way to get it back, he would let me know, but he has not said anything to me yet," replied Lucas.

Hailey remembered that Prescott told her she might need to rescue Lucas, and this might be when she was needed. She thought that maybe, with the golden Power Ring she had been given, she could find a way to help Lucas without him knowing.

"I'll be thinking of how we can help find the thief," said Hailey. "You know that I am pretty good at asking questions and snooping around until I get the answers."

"Oh, yeah, don't I know it!" said Lucas with a smile as he rolled his eyes.

"What do you mean?" asked Hailey, as she slugged Lucas in the arm.

"I know that you are like Sherlock Holmes in searching for clues, and you don't stop until you find the answer," said Lucas. "I'll just call you Sherlock Hailey." The lunch bell rang, and they headed back to their classroom.

All that afternoon Hailey thought about how she might be able to help Lucas get the Power Ring back. First, she thought that the thief was probably still in the area. The thief knew exactly where to look, but how? It would also be good if more people were looking for the thief. But how could we get the word out without alerting the thief. Then an idea came to her. When she got home, she took the golden Power Ring that Prescott had given her and went into her back yard. She looked over the back fence to make sure that no one was nearby. She turned the pointer to the symbol for mental telepathy and waited. She knew that there were lots of wild parrots in this area of Southern California, and maybe they could help. She did not have to wait very long before a green parrot with a red head flew down and perched in a tree near the pool. She felt kind of silly and was not sure what to say or if it would actually work.

"Hello, green parrot. My name is Hailey. Can you understand me?" asked Hailey.

The parrot turned to look at Hailey, cocked its head like it was listening, squawked and flew away.

"That went well," said Hailey sarcastically. She figured that she would need to try something else. She got up to telephone some friends to help when the green parrot landed in the same tree. Curious, Hailey sat down to try it again. Before she could say anything, another parrot flew to the tree, and then another until there were about twenty or thirty parrots that had landed in the trees along the fence line. What was really unusual, besides having so many parrots in the trees, was that these parrots were quiet. She tried again.

"Hello green parrot. My name is Hailey. Can you understand me?" asked Hailey.

The first parrot flew from the tree and landed on the back of the chair facing Hailey.

"See, I told you there was a girl that could talk with me," said the parrot.

Immediately, all of the other parrots broke their silence, and all started squawking at the same time.

"Quiet!" said the parrot on the chair.

Surprised and grinning from ear to ear, Hailey exclaimed, "You can hear me and understand what I am saying!"

"Of course, we can hear and understand you. Why are you talking to us?" asked the parrot.

"I need your help. My friend had a very special ring that was stolen from him. It's about this big around," said Hailey as she held up her finger and thumb to form a circle. "It's red and green and has a fire red ruby in the center."

"How can we help?" asked the parrot.

"I would like your help by having many eyes in the sky looking for the thief. The ring was stolen by a woman about twenty years old. She is slender and has black shoulder length hair and she is a little taller than me. She also has a white streak in her hair."

As Hailey was speaking to the parrot, she noticed more parrots had arrived, which maybe doubled the number of parrots in the trees. The parrot on the chair turned and faced the other parrots and asked, *"Are we ready to help this Light Bearer?"*

Without hesitation, there was a loud response of squawking from the birds. The parrot on the chair hopped around to face Hailey again, and the noise from the trees stopped.

Hailey listened in wonder at being called a Light Bearer. How could they know? There had to be something more to being a Light Bearer than she had ever imagined.

"We will be happy to help you," said the parrot. "What would you like us to do?"

Hailey told the parrot that Lucas lived near the creek and suggested that the parrots start there and spread out in an ever increasing circle looking for the woman with the white streak in her hair.

"What are we to do when we find her?" asked the parrot.

Hailey wasn't sure how to answer. Do they come back to tell me so I can call the police? Do I go and get the ring? Do I have them take the ring back?

"You need to be safe. When we find the woman, we will get the ring and return it to you," said the parrot.

It was as if the parrot knew the right thing to do.

"Yes, please get the ring and return it to me," agreed Hailey. "Thank you so much for your help."

"We are here to serve the Light Bearer," said the parrot. As if by some unseen signal, they all flew off in the direction of Lucas's house.

Just then, Hailey's mom came out of the house and excitedly said, "Did you see that flock of parrots? I have never seen so many at one time!"

"Yes, I saw them too. I was just sitting here admiring these beautiful birds in our back yard," replied Hailey with a smile.

ɛɔ ɛɔ ɛɔ

The next day at school, Lucas told Hailey that the police had a strange report.

"The police told my dad they could not get any positive identification on the blood sample found in my room, which is now a crime scene," said Lucas. "Apparently the blood sample was not human. But we already knew that."

"Did Prescott ever tell you how to find the thief?" asked Hailey

"All he said was there are many searching for the ring and to be patient," said Lucas.

"I am sure that the ring will turn up soon. Maybe it will just drop out of the sky," said Hailey with a cheerful smile.

"Thanks for trying to cheer me up," said Lucas. "I guess it is harder to believe in magic without the Power Ring."

"Is this the way a Light Bearer is supposed to be acting?" asked Hailey.

"I guess not," said Lucas. "I should have a better attitude. I should trust Prescott and be patient like he requested. Thanks, Hailey, for being such a good friend."

After school, Lucas went to the office and called his mom to see if he could go to Hailey's house.

"Is Hailey's mom going to be home?" asked his mom. Hailey was nodding her head at Lucas.

"Hailey said that her mom is home right now," answered Lucas.

He knew what was coming next and said, "I know, Mom, I promise to be home by dinner time."

Lucas hung up the phone and thanked the office secretary.

"Hailey, have you noticed that there are a lot more parrots flying around town?" asked Lucas.

"I have," said Hailey. "Maybe that's what Prescott meant when he said that there are many looking for the Power Ring."

"Wouldn't that be nice," said Lucas.

Lucas and Hailey were sitting by the pool in her backyard when Hailey said, "This is where we were when you made that water cannon and blasted that dark shadow out of the tree."

"That was pretty cool," said Lucas.

"It was also pretty scary!" exclaimed Hailey.

"Look!" said Lucas, "There's a flock of parrots flying above us."

Just as Hailey stood up and turned around to see the parrots, they made an abrupt turn and flew in the direction toward where Lucas lived. That's when they heard the loud squawking from what must have been hundreds of parrots several blocks away.

"I wonder what's going on," said Lucas.

"I supposed if you had the Power Ring," said Hailey, "you could talk to the parrots and find out what they were doing."

"Please. Don't remind me," groaned Lucas.

Hailey sat back down and watched a lone green parrot circle around behind Lucas. The parrot flew right up behind Lucas and landed on the back of his chair. Lucas was so startled by the parrot that he fell out of the chair and landed on his hands and knees. He rolled around to see the parrot on the back of the chair with his Power Ring in his beak.

"Look, Hailey! The parrot has the Power Ring," exclaimed Lucas.

The parrot looked directly at Lucas and started bobbing its head up and down.

"I think he wants to give you the Power Ring," said Hailey.

Lucas stood up and cautiously held out his hand under the parrot's beak. The parrot bobbed its head up and down again and dropped the ring into Lucas's hand. Lucas just stood there with his mouth open staring at the beautiful green parrot.

"Lucas, maybe the parrot wants to tell you something," said Hailey, smiling.

"Oh, of course," said Lucas.

"Can I listen to what the parrot has to say?" asked Hailey.

Lucas nodded as he turned the pointer on the Power Ring to the symbol for mental telepathy so Hailey could listen in on the conversation.

Lucas turned to the parrot, *"Thank you! Thank you so much! Where did you find the Power Ring?"* asked Lucas.

The parrot replied, *"My friends and I circled the town looking for the woman with black hair with the white streak, the one who stole your Power Ring. One of our best scouts saw the woman in her backyard with the ring. He watched while she would turn something on the ring and then hold it out in her hand. She did that over and over, then she stamped her foot down like she was mad."*

Lucas said, *"She must have been trying to use some power on the ring. How did you get it?"*

The parrot replied, *"We gathered together in several flocks and attacked her from behind. Three of my friends were hit very hard as she clawed at us. Sadly, they did not survive. The next flock attacked from another direction, and we were able to knock her down. That is when she dropped the Power Ring, and I heard her yelling, 'Not again! Not birds* again.' *I flew in, grabbed the ring in my beak and flew away. I have returned the Power Ring to the Light Bearer."*

"*Where did you find the woman with the streak in her black hair?*" asked Lucas.

"*Across the street from your house,*" replied the parrot. "*Is there anything else we can do for the Light Bearers?*"

"*No. Not now. Thank you for your service,*" said Lucas.

"*Call us anytime you need help,*" said the parrot as it flew away.

"I guess you were right to be concerned about Mallory," said Lucas. "I'm sure it was Senka that took the Power Ring but what was she doing in Mallory's back yard?"

"I wonder if she is staying with Mallory," said Hailey. "Have you seen anyone besides her family or maybe a different car parked in front of the house?"

"No, I don't think so," replied Lucas. "Maybe one of us should ask her tomorrow at school?"

"I'll do it," said Hailey. "I'll ask her without sounding like I'm accusing her of anything. I think I have a way to do that."

හ හ හ

When they got to school the next day, Hailey didn't have to worry about asking Mallory any questions. She was waiting for Lucas and Hailey outside their classroom. It was easy to see that she was excited about something.

"You'll never guess what happened at our house yesterday," exclaimed Mallory.

"What happened?" asked Hailey.

"Yesterday afternoon, my aunt was in our backyard by herself when a flock of wild parrots flew down and started attacking her. It was terrible!" said Mallory as she waved her arms around like flying parrots.

"That's terrible. Did she get hurt?" asked Lucas.

"She had some cuts on her hands and arms from fighting off the birds. Isn't that the craziest thing you have ever heard?" asked Mallory.

"That really is crazy!" said Lucas. "Is your aunt visiting from Texas?"

"No, she is from some place in Europe," said Mallory, "She's not actually my aunt though. I guess she is more like a cousin because she was adopted by my uncle."

Hailey asked, "How long is your aunt staying with you?"

"She's leaving sometime this morning," said Mallory. "My mom is taking her to the airport on her way to work. Do you know her, Lucas?"

"No, I don't think so," replied Lucas. "Why do you ask?"

"Well, she seems to know you," said Mallory. "She told me to tell you, 'The next time you will lose it.' Do you have any idea what she means?"

"I wish I did," replied Lucas. "Did she say anything else?"

"The only other thing she said was, 'He will not know what hit him.' She seemed kind of mad when she asked me to give you the message," said Mallory.

"What is your aunt's name?" asked Hailey.

"Senka, Senka Fontaine," replied Mallory.

The bell rang and Hailey said, "We'd better get to our seats."

Lucas had learned his lesson that in order to keep the Power Ring safe, he would need to keep it with him. He mentally turned the ring to telepathy so he could talk with Hailey through his thoughts.

"Hailey, it looks like Mallory doesn't have any idea about what's going on."

"You may be right," said Hailey.

"I still need to follow Prescott's advice to never be alone with Mallory. Senka may be using Mallory and she doesn't even know it," said Lucas.

At lunch, Hailey decided to do a little investigation on her own. When the bell rang, she hurried to the girls' bathroom and turned the pointer on her golden Power Ring to the double "S" symbol and became invisible. Someone came in behind her and she slipped out while the door was still open. She saw Mallory walking out past the lunch tables and quickly followed her. Mallory had a cell phone to her ear so Hailey got close enough to hear one side of the conversation.

"......yes, I told him exactly what you asked me to say."

"......he did not look surprised when I told him about the parrots, but Hailey was totally surprised when I told Lucas he will not know what hit him."

"Did I really look that surprised?" wondered Hailey

Mallory looked around.

"....yes, I'm alone. No one followed me."

"......yes I'm sure."

"......why do you want me to do that? What's going on?"

"......okay, but don't ask me to do anything else. I have finally made some friends and I don't want to mess that up."

"......I thought you were leaving today."

"......I know. I love you too Aunt Senka."

"......all right, see you tonight. Goodbye."

Hailey turned around and walked quickly to the girls' bathroom. Once she was alone, she released the Power Ring and became visible again. She went back to the classroom to get her lunch. She was looking for Lucas to tell him what she had heard when she realized she was stuck. She had something important to tell Lucas, but she couldn't say anything without telling Lucas how she had heard the information. Prescott said not to tell Lucas about the second Power Ring. She needed to find out why.

THIRTEEN
GHOST TOWN

When we are challenged in life, if we give all that is within us, we will have the ability and power we had not known before.

At home that afternoon, with the pointer on the ring positioned for a conversation with Prescott, Hailey asked, *"Prescott, are you there?"*

"Hello, Hailey. What can I do for you?" replied Prescott.

"Why do I need to keep the second ring a secret from Lucas?" asked Hailey.

"Only you and I know about the second ring," replied Prescott. *"If you tell anyone, including Lucas, you might be in danger or you could both be in danger. I am concerned that someone may want to use you to get to Lucas. If you have a Power Ring, you will be able to use the element of surprise to protect yourself and Lucas."*

"If he knows I have a Power Ring, he can rely on me to help," said Hailey.

"If he knows there is a second ring, he will not dig as deep as he needs to, to call upon the power within himself. He will be stronger if he must rely on himself," said Prescott.

"How will that make him stronger?" asked Hailey.

"Learning how to think clearly in the face of fear is a lesson he must master to become the powerful Light Bearer he is destined to become," replied Prescott. *"You will also have to face your fears to master yourself and become a Light Bearer."*

"Okay. I think I understand," replied Hailey.

"Are you ready to learn the next power?" asked Prescott.

"Yes. Which is the next power and how should I use it?" asked Hailey.

"It is the power of suggestion," said Prescott. *"This power is to be used with caution as with any of these powers. You may use this when you or someone else needs help to convince another."*

"You mean I can control someone's thoughts and have anyone do what I want?" asked Hailey.

"No," said Prescott firmly. *"If you did that, you would be taking away his choice or free will. Choice is a right that everyone has. What you can do is make suggestions to someone's mind and if you present a good reason that he can believe, then it becomes his choice."*

"I think I understand," said Hailey. *"If I force someone to do something against his will, it would be like taking away his freedom."*

"That is correct," replied Prescott. *"That is why you need to be very cautious. I believe that you may find this power useful very soon."*

"Which symbol on the Power Ring is used for suggestion?" asked Hailey.

"Turn the pointer to the symbol with the circle with the line through the middle. The line has a small dot on each end," said Prescott.

"Okay, now what?" asked Hailey.

"Remember that the power of persuasion must be gentle," said Prescott. *"Think of it like mist falling onto someone's mind. Imagine this mist while asking questions that might lead them to choose what you would like them to choose. You might want to*

practice this power on others before you find yourself in a situation that demands it."

The one-sided conversation that Hailey had heard from Mallory was not enough information. Hailey needed to find out more about Senka to see if Mallory was being controlled by her aunt. She decided to use the power of persuasion on Mallory to see if Mallory could shed more light on the clues that were still in the dark.

The next day at school, Hailey invited Mallory to have lunch with her. Hailey knew that Lucas would be at their table. Hailey had thought carefully how the conversation should go. Hailey turned the pointer on her Power Ring to persuasion. What happened next seemed effortless. Without any help from Hailey, Mallory steered the conversation to the parrots that attacked Senka.

"When I first saw the parrot in Lucas's backyard, I thought it was pretty," said Mallory. "But in a flock they can be mean!"

Hailey began floating questions into Mallory's mind to see if she would tell them everything she knew about her Aunt Senka.

"Did you ever figure out why they attacked your aunt," asked Hailey as she imagined the mist softly falling on Mallory.

"I'm not sure," replied Mallory. "I overheard my aunt talking to someone in her room. I think she called him Rebulus. She said that the parrots took the ring and that she would find another way to get it. But the question that just popped into my head is why she would want to hurt you, Lucas?"

"I would like to know that, too," replied Lucas.

"I love my aunt," said Mallory, "but sometimes I get a strange feeling when I'm around her. She seems to want power to control people. I'm sorry. I don't know why I'm telling you all of this. When I was talking with her yesterday, she asked me to do something."

"What was it?" asked Lucas.

"She wanted me to ask you if I could see your ring, I think she called it a power ring. And then I was to keep it," said Mallory sheepishly.

"I have this silver and green ring," said Lucas, taking it off his finger and handing it to Mallory.

165

"The only power in this ring is to remind me to choose to do what's right. You can keep it. I have another one at home."

"I would like to think that you are my friends, but I cannot take it," said Mallory.

"That's okay," said Lucas. "We are your friends, and I want you to have it. That way we will all have a power ring."

Hailey looked at Lucas and smiled as she held up her hand to show Mallory that she also had a silver and green ring like Lucas's.

ഇൻ ഇൻ ഇൻ

When Lucas got home from school, he told Prescott what he had learned about Senka and asked if there were other powers he could learn to use that would help him in his struggle with Senka and Rebulus.

Prescott said, *"There are two that I would like to teach you. The first is the power for time jumping. With the pointer toward the triangle symbol with the ball on top, think of the exact location and time to which you want to jump. It is very important that you have a clear image in your mind of where you were at the time to which you want to return."*

"Can I time jump into the future?" asked Lucas.

"It is possible," replied Prescott, *"but how are you going to know where you are in the future to place that image into your mind?"*

Lucas thought about that and realized Prescott was right and asked, "Can I try jumping back in time now?"

"Yes. Squeeze the Power Ring and hold the image of when you were walking up to the front door when you got home after school," instructed Prescott.

Lucas followed Prescott's instruction and found himself at the front door just like he had been twenty minutes earlier. Lucas opened the front door and saw his mother sitting at the kitchen table.

"Lucas, I thought you were in your room. When did you go back outside?" asked Lucas's mother.

"I went outside a short time ago," replied Lucas.

"Okay," said Lucas's mother. "I guess I didn't see you when you went outside."

Back in his room with Prescott, Lucas said, "I guess I need to practice time jumping when others are not around to see me"

"That would be best for now," replied Prescott.

"What is the other power you wanted to teach me?" asked Lucas.

"This power is only to be used with the greatest amount of care," said Prescott. *"One of the first rules I gave you was to do nothing that would change the course of someone's life. But if you feel in your heart it is right, you may use this power with limited consequences. It is the power to heal."*

"You mean if someone is sick or hurt I will have the power to make him well?" asked Lucas.

"Yes, but you must remember, before using this power, you are to search your heart. If you feel it is right, you may use the power to heal. It is the symbol with the circle and the two outward arrows. Think of the symbol as the heart in the center and love flowing outward," said Prescott.

"Is there a special way or something I must do or say to use this power," asked Lucas.

"*Turn the pointer to the symbol, wrap your hand around the Power Ring and place your closed hand and ring over the person's heart if he is sick, or on the injury if he is hurt,*" said Prescott. "*Then you are to imagine that the illness or injury is flowing out of his body out the tips of his fingers and toes. Remember, Lucas, use this with caution.*"

ဆ ဆ ဆ

For several months, Lucas and Hailey's fathers had been planning a trip to the desert to ride motorcycles and agreed to go on the day after Thanksgiving. The families left early Friday morning and arranged to explore a ghost town before going on to the camp site. The abandoned town had been built years ago at the base of a mountain, and like many ghost towns, it was built around a gold or mineral mine.

As they drove up to the ghost town, Gavin asked, "Mom, are we going to see any ghosts today?"

"Probably not," replied his mother, "but if you do, please tell me so I can take its picture."

Lucas's brother and sister and Hailey's little sister stayed close to their parents.

"Hailey and I are going to go look at that glass house up the hill," said Lucas.

"Okay, but stay out of trouble, and meet us back at the car no later than two o'clock." replied Mom.

Lucas looked at his watch and knew they had an hour and fifteen minutes. Lucas and Hailey wanted to explore the ghost town on their own without the younger kids getting in the way. They found the old house that was made out of hundreds of bottles with a clay mortar holding them together. The light from the sun came through the bottles to brighten and warm up the old one-room house. In spite of that, shortly after entering the house, they both started shivering.

"Did you feel that?" asked Hailey as they stood in the middle of the bottle house.

"Yes I did. It's Rebulus, and we need to get out of here," said Lucas.

Just then, the light from the sun was blocked out as a shadow covered the house.

"What power can you use?" asked Hailey.

Before he could answer, the rotting wood floor cracked, and Hailey and Lucas fell through the floor and dropped about eight feet into a cavern below the house. Lucas landed off balance on his feet and fell backward. Hailey then landed on top of Lucas knocking the air out of him.

"Are you okay?" asked Hailey.

It was a moment before Lucas could catch his breath and answer.

"I think so," he replied. "How are you?"

"I banged my elbow on a wooden floor board, but I'm okay," said Hailey. "Thanks for breaking my fall."

They both looked up to see if there was a way to climb back up. What they saw was the dark shadow of Rebulus the Light Thief. Lucas had experienced being surrounded by Rebulus and did not want to feel that again. Going up was not an option.

"Look!" said Hailey. "There is light coming from that opening. Let's head that way."

They both ran for the light, hoping to get out into the open where they might stand a better chance to escape the Light Thief. When they got through the short tunnel, they found themselves in a larger cavern that was lit up by light coming from pools of water scattered around the floor of the cavern. The light reflected off the ceiling which glowed and sparkled like blue diamonds.

"This seems really strange to be underneath a ghost town," whispered Hailey.

Lucas looked behind them to see the dark cloud floating over the tunnel they just came through.

"It's not coming after us," said Lucas. "It's almost like he's pushing us deeper into the cavern."

"We can't go back," said Hailey.

"Well, let's hope that going toward the light will get us out of here," said Lucas.

The path seemed to take them downward, and Lucas could not remember in which direction they were headed. It was either deeper into the

mountain or heading down to the ravine on the lower side of the ghost town. They had to walk along a narrow path around the pools of water and along the edge of the cavern. The path turned right, leading away from the pools and down another tunnel. Lucas turned and saw a faint glow that he hoped was their escape route.

"I see a light," said Lucas. "It's this way. I can feel a breeze on our backs blowing the cool air outside."

Lucas had only gone about twenty feet when he heard a muffled scream from Hailey. Lucas spun around. Hailey was gone!

"Hailey, are you okay? Where are you?" shouted Lucas.

Lucas could only hear his own echo and started running back up the tunnel. When he got back to the dimly lit cavern he was shocked to see Senka on the other side of the pools of water and Rebulus the Light Thief blocking the far opening.

"Where's Hailey?" demanded Lucas.

"Did you lose your friend?" asked Senka sarcastically.

Lucas was trying to think which power he could use against Rebulus and Senka, but he had to find Hailey first. That's when he heard a voice in his head.

"*I'm up here, Lucas,*" said Hailey.

"*Up where?*" asked Lucas.

Lucas took another step out of the tunnel and looked up to see that Hailey was inside a metal cage suspended from the top of the cavern.

"Lucas, don't try anything foolish," said Senka. "You know what I want. Give me the Power Ring, and I will let your friend go free."

"How can I trust you?" asked Lucas.

"You don't have much of a choice," replied Senka with a sneer.

Lucas saw Rebulus out of the corner of his eye getting closer as Senka took several steps closer to Lucas and held out her hand.

Lucas heard Prescott's voice in his head telling him, *"You must trust Hailey."*

Before he could ask why, he heard Hailey's voice in his mind.

"Lucas, I have an idea on how to get out of this cage but you have to create a distraction," said Hailey.

"What are you going to do?" asked Lucas.

"Just trust me," replied Hailey, as she turned the pointer on her Power Ring to the symbol for invisibility.

Lucas saw a large rock on the far side of the cavern. Using the telekinetic power, he lifted the rock from the ground and threw it toward Rebulus. Rebulus moved out of the path of the rock as it bounced off the wall and splashed into a pool of water near Rebulus. That's when the cage came crashing down. Lucas turned to look to see if Hailey was hurt, but the cage was open and Hailey was nowhere to be seen.

"Where did she go?" yelled Senka. "What did you do with her?"

"I didn't do anything!" yelled Lucas. "What did YOU do with her?"

Lucas was just as surprised as Senka at Hailey's disappearance. Then without warning, Rebulus flew to the cage and pushed it toward Lucas. The open door on the cage swallowed Lucas before he had a chance to consider what to do. The door slammed shut and Lucas was locked inside.

Senka walked over to the cage with a look of triumph and said, "Hand me the Power Ring little Lucas. You are trapped and there is no way out."

Lucas thought that if he could just jump back in time to when they walked into the bottle house, they could avoid this as if it had never happened.

"*I think that's a great idea,*" said Hailey. "*Can you really do that?*"

Lucas looked around but could not see Hailey anywhere.

"*Yes, I can. Where are you?*" asked Lucas.

"Come on, Lucas," snarled Senka. "Just give me the ring, or you will be locked in the cage at the bottom of this pool. This will be your water tomb. I'll just get the ring after you have breathed your last breath."

Lucas heard Hailey again in his head, *"Lucas, I'm ready to go swimming. How about you? Are you ready?"*

"Sure. But I won't go without you. We can only jump time together if I am holding your hand," said Lucas.

"Trust me and don't give her the ring," said Hailey.

Gathering his courage, Lucas looked at Senka with the most defiant look he could put on and said, "I am never going to give you or Rebulus the ring."

"Have it your way," said Senka. "Push him in."

Lucas took a huge gulp of air just as Rebulus pushed the cage into the largest pool with a tremendous splash. Senka laughed as she watched it sink to the bottom. The cage sank about twenty feet and landed on the rocks at the bottom of the pool. That's when Lucas felt Hailey's hand slip into his.

"*Can we please time jump right now, Lucas?*" said Hailey. "*I need to breathe real soon!*"

Lucas remembered Prescott's warning and focused very carefully on visualizing Hailey and himself standing in front of the bottle house and turned the pointer to the symbol for time jumping. He squeezed hard on the ring. He felt like his lungs would burst.

"*Any time now,*" pleaded Hailey.

Instantly, Lucas and Hailey were standing in front of the bottle house in dry clothes. Just as Lucas reached for the door knob, he had a feeling of dread.

"I don't think we should go in there," said Hailey.

"I had the same feeling," said Lucas. "Let's go find the rest of our family."

FOURTEEN
DESERT SERPENTS

Demand more from yourself than anyone else could ever expect.

Lucas and Hailey's fathers pulled their trailers off the highway and drove into the desert about a mile. They found a spot where there were several other trailers parked, away from the noise and lights of the highway. They set up camp so they could get a couple hours of riding before dark. The dads rode their motorcycles, and Lucas, Hailey and Gavin all rode their quads.

"Let's start with Gavin being the leader," said Lucas's dad, "and then Hailey and then Lucas."

Hailey's dad said, "Remember, being the leader doesn't mean racing and losing control, but leading the rest of the riders in safety."

They each took turns being the leader with the instruction to be sure the path was safe for those following and to watch for oncoming traffic.

When it was Hailey's turn to lead, she came up on a slight rise and skidded to an abrupt stop which sent a cloud of dust spraying in the air.

Lucas was next to stop and asked, "What's wrong Hailey?"

"What's wrong is a pair of rattlesnakes on the trail," said Hailey. "I hate snakes! I hate snakes! I hate snakes!"

The snakes were only about six feet away. Both snakes coiled and began rattling their tails when Hailey's dad rode up and came to a stop. After a few seconds, the snakes slithered away from the trail.

"I thought they might strike, but I guess you scared them," said Hailey.

Her dad replied, "Rattlesnakes have heat sensors below their nostrils. They probably detected the heat from the engines and determined that they were in danger."

"I forgot that there might be snakes here in the desert," said Hailey. "I'm ready to head back to camp."

After they got back to camp, Gavin got out his remote controlled car and started running it around the camp area.

"Gavin," asked his mother, "can you please race your car away from where I am trying to fix dinner?" Then she added, "Lucas, will you please make sure that Gavin doesn't go too far."

"Sure, Mom," replied Lucas.

Lucas was watching Gavin race his car in and around the clumps of dry grass when he heard the whine of other remote controlled cars. Lucas looked to where he heard the noise and saw some other kids his age racing their cars toward them.

When they got closer, one of the boys said, "Hey, cool car."

"Thanks," said Gavin. "I like yours, too."

The tallest boy said, "My name is Trenton, and these are my cousins, Kendall and Carter. What are your names?"

Lucas spoke up, "My name is Lucas, and this is my brother Gavin and my friend Hailey."

"Where do you guys live?" asked Trenton.

"We live in Orange County," said Lucas.

"Where's that?" asked Carter.

"We live about ten miles from Disneyland," replied Hailey. "How about you guys?"

"We live on the Central Coast," replied Kendall. "It looks like you guys have been riding today."

"Our dads are riding their motorcycles, and we are riding on quads," said Lucas.

"We are riding our quads, too," said Carter.

All of a sudden, Kendall let out a scream. Everyone looked over at her to see several tarantulas at her feet.

"Get them away from me," shouted Kendall.

"Be still," said Trenton. "If you don't frighten them, they won't bother you."

"Well, they ARE bothering me," said Kendall.

Trenton found a small board and got two of the hairy spiders to climb onto the wooden plank. Carter scooped up the third tarantula in his hat, and the boys carefully carried them about twenty feet away from Kendall.

Kendall and Hailey were comparing their fear of spiders and snakes when they heard Hailey's mother calling everyone to dinner. The kids said their goodbyes and Trenton suggested that they all might ride together the next day.

ຄະ ຄະ ຄະ

After dinner, Lucas and Hailey were sitting in chairs away from the fire and talking about what happened at the ghost town. Their parents were sitting by the fire making s'mores with the other kids.

"I'm beginning to remember what had happened today at the glass house," said Lucas.

"Me, too," said Hailey. "It's kind of like a dream. Senka and Rebulus were there. We got away because you were able to takes us back in time before anything bad happened to us."

"Yes, that was a new power that Prescott taught me," said Lucas.

As his memory came back to him in bits and pieces, Lucas tried to put together the events leading up to being dropped in the water.

"Hailey, I'm still a little fuzzy on what happened. Where were you after you escaped from the cage?" asked Lucas.

Hailey was torn between following what Prescott had said and telling Lucas.

"Tell me what?" asked Lucas

Hailey had forgotten that they had given each other permission to hear each other's thoughts and Lucas had heard her. She also knew that Lucas had created a clever escape plan, which is what Prescott wanted from Lucas. That's when they both heard Prescott in their minds.

"Lucas and Hailey, I heard and saw what happened today and you both did very well," said Prescott. *"I am very pleased with your actions. Lucas, your test was to see how strong and smart you can be when you are faced with an adversary like Senka or Rebulus. Both of you were able to overcome your fears and work together to escape. Hailey, you may show Lucas the gift I have given you."*

Hailey reached into her pocket and withdrew the golden ring and said, "This is how I disappeared when the cage came down. I had to let you figure out our escape. I was still in the cage, but I couldn't hold your hand until we were safely under water or you would have been invisible as well."

Lucas began smiling, which was a big relief to Hailey. She was afraid that Lucas would somehow be resentful that she had a power ring too.

Lucas picked up on her thoughts and said, "I'm not jealous. I'm glad to know that you have a ring, too. Every Light Bearer should have one."

"This means we can work together," said Lucas, "but we should never let Senka or Rebulus find out that you have a Power Ring as well."

Hailey explained to Lucas how Prescott had given her the ring from the hidden compartment in the golden box he had found under the bridge. She told him about using her Power Ring to listen to Mallory and to enlist the help of the parrots to recover Lucas's Power Ring. They got another good laugh talking about the parrots and their swooping in on Senka.

Lucas and Hailey did not see the rattlesnakes coiled in the sand behind them. They did not see or hear them slither away toward a dark slender figure sitting on a rock. Lucas and Hailey did not hear the desert serpents tell what they had heard and seen near the fire. But Lucas and Hailey did hear a lone wolf howl in the distance.

"I'm getting cold," said Hailey. "Let's move closer to the fire."

℘ ℘ ℘

The next morning Kendall's father came over to introduce himself and said that this was his first time to the area. He explained that their kids had met the night before and suggested that the kids could ride together. They all agreed to meet at ten o'clock at the trail entrance between their campsites.

Lucas's dad took the lead to show the new riders the different trails and some of the fun jumps. The dads wanted a little more of a challenge and asked the kids to stay closer to camp while they rode toward the hills beyond the camp.

Lucas, Trenton and Carter created their own track and told Hailey and Kendall to follow them.

The girls followed for a while but got tired of the dust and stopped. Pointing her finger, Hailey said to Kendall, "Let's see what's over that ridge."

Hailey and Kendall took off in the opposite direction and stopped when they got to the top of the ridge near some trees.

"Do you see that?" asked Kendall. "There's something reflecting in the sun."

Hailey looked to where Kendall was pointing and saw a rainbow of bright colors and said, "Let's check it out."

They rode down the hill and got off the quads to get a closer look at the object.

"It looks like a glass prism that is reflecting a rainbow," said Hailey. "I wonder who left it here?"

As Hailey bent down to pick up the prism, rattlesnakes seemed to come out of nowhere and moved toward the girls. There had to be at least five or six snakes.

Hailey turned her Power Ring to the symbol for mental telepathy but said out loud, "What are you doing here? What do you want?"

"Why are you talking to the rattlesnakes?" asked Kendall.

Hailey heard one snake reply to her question, *"If you are talking to us, you must be the one the wolf wants. We heard you and the boy talking last night, and we have a surprise for you."*

Without any warning, two of the snakes struck Hailey and buried their fangs deep into her legs above her boots. Hailey screamed in pain and fell to the ground.

She heard the snake say, *"That should keep you still until the wolf arrives."*

Kendall started to back away in fear as the snakes moved in her direction. Before they could attack Kendall, Hailey turned the pointer on the Power Ring to stop time, and the snakes froze with their mouths open and their fangs exposed. Kendall had tripped backward and was frozen half way to the ground. All movement and sound ceased as Hailey lay on the ground in pain.

In her mind, Hailey pleaded, *"Lucas, I need help right now! I have been bitten by rattlesnakes! Please hurry!"*

"I'm on my way," assured Lucas.

Lucas had seen where Hailey and Kendall had disappeared and told the other boys to go find their dads and bring them to the top of the ridge with the two Joshua trees. Lucas had reached Hailey in less than two minutes. He jumped off his quad and ran to where Hailey lay on the ground. He saw that Hailey had stopped time and immediately grabbed all of the rattlesnakes and hurled them as far as he could.

Hailey felt lightheaded and was losing her strength to stay conscious as she whispered to Lucas, "Senka is coming. She did this."

Hailey's legs were starting to swell because of the venom, and she was having trouble breathing. Lucas thought back to Prescott's instruction and felt in his heart that he should use the Power Ring to heal Hailey.

"Lie still and try to remain calm," said Lucas as he pulled the Power Ring from his pocket and turned the pointer for the symbol to heal. He closed his hand tight over the ring and placed it over the first snake bite. Lucas closed his eyes and forced his mind to see the venom freely flowing out of Hailey's toes. He had to heal Hailey before she lost consciousness and let go of the Power Ring allowing time started again. He moved his Power Ring to the other leg and again mentally saw the venom flow out of Hailey's body.

After a few moments, Lucas opened his eyes when he heard Hailey say, "Lucas, thank you. I don't know how you did it, but I am starting to feel better again."

Lucas got up and stood behind Kendall and said, "I'll tell how I did it later. The snakes are gone and before Senka or anyone else gets here, let go of your Power Ring. I'll catch Kendall so she doesn't fall too hard."

The sounds around Lucas and Hailey started to increase as Kendall finished her fall. Lucas caught Kendall, and she continued where she had left off with her wild screaming. She was still kicking her legs as she tried to crawl backward up the hill.

"Where are they?" asked Kendall. "Where are the snakes?"

"Sometimes the desert plays tricks on the mind," said Lucas.

"But I saw them," said Kendall.

"In the desert we often see things that are not really there. Maybe it was a mirage and you were affected by the heat," said Lucas as he looked at Hailey and winked.

Hailey grabbed her helmet and jumped up as she said, "Let's go back to camp and get some lunch. I am hungry."

FIFTEEN

WATER TOMB

You must become the rock the river cannot wash away. Like the rock, remain steadfast and immoveable.

Lucas, Hailey and their dads had ridden about five miles from camp on a well-worn trail. They made note of the rock markers along the trail to find their way back. They stopped to rest and to drink some water.

Hailey's dad Mark said, "Those storm clouds north of us look really threatening. We should head back."

"Look at that cool cloud that looks like a mushroom," said Lucas. "What is that?"

"Those are called cumulonimbus rain clouds," replied Hailey's dad. "That mushroom cloud is called a hammerhead because the top looks like a blacksmith's anvil where the hammer comes down. If we don't get back to the trailers, we are going to be hammered with rain."

Lucas's dad said, "Because there is a lot of rain from these clouds, there is a chance of flash floods in the ravines. That's the other reason we should head back."

Hailey's dad started back on the trail with Hailey, Lucas and his dad following them. After riding for a few minutes, they reached the top of a ridge, and Hailey asked if she could stop to take some pictures of the storm clouds and lightning. She and Lucas wanted to do a school report of the desert with photos, and Hailey promised they would only be one or two minutes behind, so the dads agreed and said they would ride to the top of the next ridge. There were a few lightning strikes in the distance, and Hailey really wanted to capture a lightning bolt.

After a few photos, Lucas said, "Hailey, we need to go."

"Wait just a minute, Lucas. I want to get a lightning strike, and I need to hold the camera still while I take a time exposure," said Hailey.

Lucas counted the seconds between the lightning and the time he heard the thunder. The time was about ten seconds, so he estimated the lightning was about two miles away.

"Okay, I got my picture," said Hailey. "We can go."

She stuffed her camera into her jacket, and they both put on their helmets. They waved at their dads to show they were following. They had only gone about a quarter mile when lightning struck a low ridge over the trail in front of them, and some boulders rolled down to block the trail. Lucas had kept the Power Ring in his pocket so they could talk to one another in their minds.

"Hailey, we need to find another way," said Lucas. *"Come back toward me, and let's cross this ravine and go back on the other side."*

Hailey turned around and followed Lucas down the ravine and back up the other side. The thunder clouds were getting closer, and they saw the heavy rain on the mountains to the north.

Lucas heard his dad calling on the walkie-talkie. *"Lucas, do you read me?"* Lucas stopped and got out his walkie-talkie.

"I hear you, Dad. We are okay," said Lucas. "The lightning knocked some boulders in front of us and blocked the main trail. We are coming back on the South trail."

"Okay, but keep in touch," said Dad.

The wind from the storm was blowing dust into the air making it difficult to see the trail. Lucas did not see that the trail ahead curved to the left. By the time he saw the bend it was too late to stop or turn, and Lucas flew over the edge of a ravine with his quad.

"Hailey, you need to stop!" said Lucas quickly, hoping she got his message.

Time seemed to slow down, but Lucas knew he was approaching the river bed at the speed of gravity. He pushed himself away from the quad and positioned himself to land in the sand. The quad landed with a thud, and Lucas forced himself into a ball so that he continued rolling when he hit the ground. As he rolled to a stop, he thought his fall must have looked comical, like something from a Saturday morning cartoon. It all happened so fast he had no time to even think about the Power Ring, let alone what power to use to stop the fall.

"Lucas!" shouted Hailey. "Are you hurt?"

Lucas lay there for a few seconds before he decided that the soft sand in the river bed had saved him from major injury, and he stood up to brush himself off.

"What happened?" asked Hailey. "Are you hurt?"

"I'm okay," replied Lucas. "Just a little shook up."

Hailey turned off her engine and slid down the eight foot bank to the river bed to check on Lucas. He seemed to be okay and took off his helmet.

"I am glad I was wearing my helmet," said Lucas. "But how am I going to get the quad back up onto the trail."

"Can you use the Power Ring to move it?" asked Hailey.

"I suppose so," replied Lucas. "I guess this is in the area of helping others without being selfish."

Lucas and Hailey got the quad turned over on its wheels and checked to see if he could start the engine. Lucas tried several times but it would not start.

"Something must have happened in the fall. We'll probably have to tow it back," said Lucas. "I'll call my dad."

Lucas pulled out the walkie-talkie to call his dad, but there was no response or even static from the speaker. That's when he realized that the walkie-talkie had broken when he fell. The wind coming down the canyon was getting much cooler and they knew that the rain was getting closer.

"We need to get out of here," said Lucas. "If there's a flash flood in this river bed, we'll probably be washed away and drown."

The rolling thunder was getting louder, and they knew that the rain was getting closer. That last thunder clap reminded Lucas of the time he was lying on the grass in the park on the Forth of July. The fireworks were exploding all around, and he could feel the force of the explosion pounding on his chest. Lucas pulled out the Power Ring and turned the pointer to the three arrows. He was just getting ready to use the power of telekinesis to lift the quad back to the trail when he heard a familiar voice.

"Hello, Lucas, we meet again."

Lucas looked up to see the wolf standing on the top of the bank about twenty feet away.

"Did you miss me, Lucas?" asked Senka. Her voice was like venom dripping from her tongue.

"No. Why would I miss you?" replied Lucas. "Why can't you leave us alone?"

"I'll leave you alone when you give me what I want," replied Senka.

"I'm glad you brought your girlfriend," said Senka. "She, too, has a treasure that will soon be mine."

"I am not his girlfriend, Senka," countered Hailey loudly. She wasn't sure if she was being loud to be heard over the noise of the thunder or if she was responding to the fear of challenging a wolf.

"Oh, your girlfriend knows my name. What else does she know about me? Did my niece Mallory tell on me?" asked Senka.

Hailey stood up as tall as she could and said, "I know you can't use the Power Ring because it can only be used for good. I know that Mallory didn't say anything about you, and I think you are wicked for using her to get to us. And I know that you don't like birds," shouted Hailey.

"Oh, you are a spirited girl. You are right on everything except one," said Senka. "I can use the Power Ring. I just need to change the fire crystal to a storm crystal. My friend Rebulus found a storm crystal for me. You remember Rebulus, don't you, Lucas?"

"You know what I want, Lucas," said Senka. "I want the Power Ring. This time I am not going to fall for your round rock trick."

Lucas kept thinking about the comment that Prescott had made to him about all of the evil in the world. He needed to keep himself away from evil and maintain the virtue of a Light Bearer. Prescott had said, *'You must become the rock the river cannot wash away.'* That gave him an idea.

Lucas would often call on Prescott for advice but this time he did not. He was surprised to hear Prescott in his mind.

"Lucas, do you need help?" asked Prescott with concern.

"I think I've got this," replied Lucas.

"Lucas, I believe in you," said Prescott. *"If you give all that is within you, when the moment demands, you will be brought to an ability and power that you have not known before,"*

"Hailey," said Lucas in her mind, *"If I don't do something right now to get rid of Senka, she's going to keep coming after me. When I yell 'run', I want*

you to turn and start running down river and get behind that big boulder."

Hailey turned around to see the boulder and asked, *"Is it the big one on the right?"*

"That's the one," replied Lucas.

"Girlfriend, you can look around, but there is no place to go that I can't catch you. There is no escaping this time," mocked Senka. "It looks like you two are trapped. There are no birds, or bears or bees around to help you out this time."

Lucas was thinking of what he could say to stall Senka a little longer.

"The Power Ring was made to be used only for good with the fire crystal," said Lucas. "The crystal is locked in place and cannot be removed. Even if you could remove it, without the crystal, the ring is useless."

"Oh, you are such a silly boy," said Senka. "I can smash the crystal to remove it. I have my own magic to lock the storm crystal into the Power Ring. Then, I will have power over you. I will have power over you and all the other Light Bearers. The Light Bearers will be destroyed."

There were a few large rain drops being blown on the wind, and Lucas heard the rumbling for which he had been stalling.

"I will give you the Power Ring but, I will not give you the power!" yelled Lucas.

"You can't stop me!" snapped Senka.

Lucas slowly pulled the Power Ring from his pocket, and then, with all of his strength, he threw the Power Ring high into the air toward the middle of the river bed and yelled, "Run Hailey!"

Lucas and Hailey turned around and began running away from Senka toward the boulder.

The boulder was about fifty yards away, and they struggled to run in the soft sand. They saw the flash of lightning behind them light up the darkness from the storm clouds and heard the thunder almost immediately.

The lightning was so close that the sound waves from the thunder slammed into their backs and pushed them closer to the rock. They ran with all their might, but they did not dare to look behind them.

Lucas grabbed Hailey's hand and yelled, "Hold on tight and run as fast as you can!"

The laughing sound that Senka made transformed into a loud blood-curdling howl as she jumped down from the bank to retrieve the Power Ring. Senka picked up the Power Ring in her mouth and turned to leap back up onto the bank when the flash flood from the storm surged down the ravine and crashed into the wolf. She was thrown against a rock and then tossed over Lucas's quad before landing hard onto the river bed. The quad was lifted by the powerful force of the raging river, and it came down with a mighty crash onto the wolf's head. More rocks were carried by the furious torrent of water and piled over the quad. The rocks and the river became the watery tomb for Senka.

Lucas and Hailey dashed behind the boulder only seconds before the full force of the flash flood hit them. Lucas had hoped that the boulder was stronger than the river's current and they both grabbed on to a tree root that was extending out of the bank. The boulder became their shield as the roaring water swirled around and splashed over the top. They were soaked as the muddy water started rising and lifted them toward the bank. After several minutes, the water level receded slowly, and Lucas thought about the last thing that Grandma Ellie had said to him. *"Remember, as a Light Bearer, you must be stronger than the storm."*

At first he thought that she meant a storm like the rain and the flashflood they had just experienced. Then he realized she probably meant that the storm was the evil like Senka, and he needed to be stronger than the storm of evil in the world.

Lucas asked, "Are you all right, Hailey?"

"Yes, but I'm wet and cold," replied Hailey.

The water in the ravine was reduced to a small stream, and they noticed that the wind was now blowing eastward. The clouds gave way to patches of blue sky, and the afternoon sun broke through to make the most beautiful rainbow they had ever seen.

"We need to get back to the quads and back on the trail," said Lucas.

They came out from the protective pocket behind the boulder and looked back at Lucas's overturned quad in the middle of the stream. There were large rocks piled around the quad, and it was covered with sand. As they got near the wreckage, they saw the paw of the wolf sticking out one side of the rocks. On the other side of the rock pile they saw the wolf's mouth. Hailey saw something red sparkling under several inches of water near the wolf.

"Lucas, look! There's your Power Ring!' exclaimed Hailey.

Lucas reached down and pulled the ring out of the water. Except for some teeth marks, it appeared to be undamaged. Lucas turned the pointer to the three arrows and lifted the quad out of the river bed and back up to the trail behind Hailey's quad. With the quad removed from the river bed, they saw the motionless body of the wolf partially buried in the sand.

"We should give her a proper burial," said Hailey.

"You're right," agreed Lucas.

Lucas used the power of telekinesis and removed the sand underneath the wolf, and she slowly sank below the river bed. Lucas then moved the sand back over Senka and made a pile of rocks over the burial spot.

"We need to go find our families. I am sure they are worried about us," said Hailey. They climbed up the bank to the trail and tied a rope between the quads to pull Lucas's back to camp. They had gone about a mile when they met their dads coming toward them on the South trail.

When they came together, Lucas's dad asked, "Are you guys okay? We saw that there was a flash flood in the ravine."

Lucas and Hailey looked at each other and grinned. "We ran into a bit of trouble, but it was nothing we couldn't handle," said Lucas. "My quad is going to need a few repairs, though."

🕉 🕉 🕉

The following week Hailey was hanging out with Lucas and Prescott on the trampoline. They were talking about the adventures they had had in the desert and their run-in with Senka.

Prescott said, *"Both of you have shown me by your actions that you are ready to follow in the footsteps of the Light Bearers that have traveled this way before you. Lucas and Hailey, I believe you are ready to learn the last symbols on the Power Rings. I will not always be here to help you."*

"What do you mean?" asked Lucas.

"Both of you are getting to the point where you can conduct yourselves in a manner befitting a Light Bearer, and my training will be complete," said Prescott. "There are other Master Light Bearers you will meet. They too have important things to teach you"

"Who are they," asked Lucas.

"You have already met some of them. They have been watching over you. Be patient my young friends and you will meet them all," said Prescott. "You each have great potential to become powerful Light Bearers."

"What do you mean by powerful?" asked Lucas.

"The remaining symbols on the ring are the most powerful," said Prescott. "Rebulus will not stop his efforts to get the Power Ring from you to work his evil plans."

"What should we do?" asked Hailey.

"Always be on your guard," replied Prescott, "and remember that the greatest power will come from your heart. As your training continues, you *must learn to master all of these powers so you will be ready for the battle that is yet to come."*

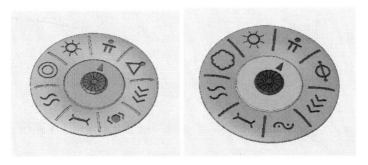

Lucas's Power Ring   Hailey's Power Ring

About the Authors

Hugo Haselhuhn lives in San Luis Obispo County and has a passion to create a positive influence for good in the lives of others. Hugo has incorporated lessons to strengthen human relations shared in this story and the readers are learning through the eyes and experiences of the characters.

This book series began as a request from his co-author, eight-year-old grandson, Luke Cowdell, who wanted help in writing a "chapter book". Luke is an avid reader with an active imagination. He is also a deep thinker and asks questions seemingly beyond his years.